S0-AZS-158

ADAPTED BY TED CONNER

Story by Bryan Singer & David
Hayter and Zak Penn

Screenplay by: Dan Harris & Mike Dougherty

BANTAM BOOKS

RL: AGES 9 AND UP

X-MEN 2

A Bantam Book/March 2003

ISBN: 0-553-48776-0

Visit us on the Web! www.randomhouse.com/kids
Educators and librarians, for a variety of teaching tools, visit us at
www.randomhouse.com/teachers

Published simultaneously in the United States and Canada

Bantam Books is an imprint of Random House Children's Books, a division of Random House, Inc. BANTAM BOOKS and the rooster colophon are registered trademarks of Random House, Inc.

PRINTED IN THE UNITED STATES OF AMERICA

OPM 10 9 8 7 6 5 4 3 2 1

MUTANTS.

SINCE THE DISCOVERY OF THEIR EXISTENCE, THEY HAVE BEEN REGARDED WITH FEAR, SUSPICION, AND OFTEN HATRED. ACROSS THE PLANET, DEBATE RAGES: ARE MUTANTS THE NEXT LINK IN THE EVOLUTIONARY CHAIN . . . OR SIMPLY A NEW SPECIES OF HUMANITY, FIGHTING FOR THEIR SHARE OF THE WORLD?

EITHER WAY, ONE FACT HAS BEEN HISTORICALLY PROVEN: SHARING THE WORLD HAS NEVER BEEN HUMANITY'S DEFINING ATTRIBUTE.

CHAPTER ONE

THE WHITE HOUSE

"'We are not enemies, but friends. We must not be enemies. Though passion may have strained, it must not break our bonds of affection.'" The young woman smiled at the camera-toting tour group as she led them through the carpeted halls of the White House that were open to the public. She stopped in front of a portrait of Abraham Lincoln. "Lincoln said that in his inaugural address as our nation's sixteenth president." She smiled more broadly. "It's one of my favorites."

As the tour group admired the portrait, the young woman began leading them to a security checkpoint. Armed Secret Service agents were watching closely as they approached. Metal detectors crammed the small space, and cameras trained down on it from above.

"If you'll please have your tickets ready, we'll begin the tour," the guide said, gesturing to the metal detectors. The tourists filed through obediently—everyone except a non-descript man in a baseball cap and a long trench coat. As the others went through the checkpoint, he stepped to the side and turned the corner. A janitor's closet was there, just out of sight of the security officers. The closet door was open slightly.

He darted inside. Moments later, *bamf!* a flash of light beamed out from under the closet door. Smoke seeped through the doorjamb. The door cracked open and he stepped outside.

He wasn't an ordinary man.

He was Nightcrawler.

As he headed down the hall, away from the tour group, a hand grabbed his shoulder. He turned, careful to keep his head bent down.

"I'm sorry, sir," said one of the security officers. "Are you lost?"

Nightcrawler nodded, staying shielded. He was there to do something, but what it was danced around his mind, never letting him fully grasp it. A beat went by and then he looked up, revealing his face. The face of a demon. Yellow, dilated eyes surrounded by skin so blue it appeared black bore into the security officer. His teeth and the whites of his eyes glinted.

"What—" Gasping, the security officer reached for his pistol. But he was too slow. From behind the agent's head,

Nightcrawler's forked tail reached up and *whish!* wrapped around the gun, throwing it to the ground. He flipped the officer over. Then, fingers curled and teeth bared like an animal, he ran down the White House corridor at full speed.

—X2—

Something bad was going down. Something very bad. Agent Fabrizio pressed his earpiece closer, his heart racing. "Perimeter breach at visitors' checkpoint!" screeched the White House Secret Service agent on the other end.

Agent Soltis ran up to him. "Multiple subjects!" he cried, his eyes ricocheting left and right. "I just went to shoot it— and there was another one!"

Agent Fabrizio motioned for him to follow and the two men raced into the Oval Office.

"Mr. President, security breach." Fabrizio waved away President McKenna's bewildered assistant, Jackie, and grabbed the president. "Let's get him out to the car!" he yelled to Soltis.

Before they could reach the exit, three more agents swarmed into the room, surrounding them. "The exit's not clear!" shouted a rookie, Agent Morris. "We don't know how many there are!"

More Secret Service agents crowded into the room and formed a circle around President McKenna. All of them had their guns drawn, pointing toward the several doorways into the room.

Alarms blared. Radios broadcast loud, unintelligible static. And then shots rang out directly outside the Oval Office. Women shrieked. Men screamed.

"There's something in the corridor!" a panicked agent said.

"Shelter!" barked Fabrizio.

The agents rushed President McKenna toward an adjoining room. But the room's door burst open before they reached it, and agents outfitted in SWAT gear spilled into the Oval Office.

"Negative!" one of the SWAT agents shouted at Fabrizio. "Not clear."

Agent Fabrizio had to look only once at the terrified president. "Lock this place down!" he commanded, adrenaline surging into his bloodstream. Agents began closing all the doors in the room. Fabrizio knew that agents would be in place outside the doors as well.

Fear enveloped him as gunfire erupted in the White House corridor. *Bamf! Bamf! Bamf!* There was a deafening, sickening slap of something making contact with human flesh. Fabrizio raised his gun, watching the door.

Then he heard a noise from above him. Footsteps. Were they an agent's? Or an enemy's?

Wham! The west door burst open, slamming an agent to

the ground. Thick smoke began filling the room. Agents stumbled in, coughing and wiping their tearing eyes.

Then Agent Morris came in—but not on his feet. He was wrapped in the clutches of a giant, slimy tail.

Bamf! The reptile mutant attacker was on the ceiling. His tail unfurled and Agent Morris dropped to the ground.

"My God," said President McKenna, the blood draining from his face.

Agent Fabrizio was frozen as the mutant practically flew around the room. A whirling tail knocked one of the agents in the face. Fabrizio could barely make out glazed yellow eyes and blue lips as the mutant destroyed agent after agent with a flick of its tail.

Bamf! Bamf! Bamf! He held on to his gun, trying to focus, and waited for the cold scaly skin to slap hard into his body and send him hurtling across the room.

—X2—

With a flick of his tail, Nightcrawler pulled a knife from his boot and flipped it into his clawed hand. Earlier he had tied a long red ribbon to its hilt. He couldn't remember why.

The man pinned underneath him on the mahogany desk looked up at him, panic washing across his seasoned features. His shirt was torn, and his watch hung broken from his wrist.

Papers had scattered to the floor. The acrid smell of smoke filled the air. Sirens wailed.

Nightcrawler raised the knife. *BANG!* A bullet ripped though his shoulder.

"Aarghhhh!" he screamed, clutching himself in pain as the agent who had shot him lowered his gun. Suddenly his eyes dilated, then snapped back to normal. He shook himself. The pain stirred something inside of him. The hazy feeling was gone. He knew where he was now. And why he was there.

The man underneath him was the president of the United States. And he, Kurt Wagner, aka Nightcrawler, had nearly killed him.

Bamf! With one final flick of his tail and a shower of smoke, he fled the Oval Office.

"What the hell was that?" he heard President McKenna say in a shaky voice.

His answer was there in front of him, on the knife that Nightcrawler had stabbed straight into the center of the president's desk.

A knife with a ribbon that had these words inscribed in black letters:

MUTANT FREEDOM NOW

CHAPTER TWO

ALBERTA, CANADA

Snow had fallen for days. An endless white-covered plain lay spread out in front of Logan, dwarfing him. He glanced back over his shoulder at the long trail of footsteps—his footsteps—that vanished into the already-crossed distance. Then he forged onward. Afternoon turned to night. Night turned cold and dark. Logan kept walking.

When he reached the top of the mountain crest the next morning, he paused. Across the snow he could make out the Alkali Lake Industrial Complex, and next to it, some sort of hydroelectric dam. It was the place Professor Xavier had told him about . . . the place where the X-Men had found him. Then his eyes lit on an abandoned military building, half buried in the snow. The structure was rusted and corroded from years of obvious neglect.

A wolf appeared in its doorway, watching him.

Logan walked toward the front of the abandoned building, toward what had once been a grand arched entrance. Now the door flapped open and closed with the wind.

The wolf stood there, growling.

Logan stepped forward and the wolf ran inside.

Logan looked around. *This could be it.* Professor X had told him he might find some answers here. He was ready. He closed his eyes, took a deep breath, and passed through.

He found himself in an open courtyard. The building lay around him in bits and pieces. A pile of ruins. There was no building intact. The doorway he had entered was part of a decaying façade.

Nothing was left of this place.

—X2—

The kids peered at the science museum's diorama. It was a winter landscape. A mother wolf with blood on her teeth was angrily protecting her young from a Neanderthal hunter—who had blood on *his* teeth.

Storm pointed to the diorama. "Neanderthals. It was once believed they were wiped out by years of conflict with a more advanced branch of humanity"—she gestured toward an exhibit on human evolution—"called Cro-Magnon man. But new evidence in our own DNA suggests that these two species may have interbred."

She paused in her delivery and glanced over at Artie. At twelve years old he was one of the most likable of Professor X's students—and also one of the most impulsive. He was staring at the display alongside a small girl with Kool-Aid stains on her dress.

Artie smiled at her. The little girl scowled and stuck out her tongue. Artie returned the gesture—except *his* tongue was black and forked. Storm smothered a laugh as the girl raced off to find her parents.

"Eventually these species evolved into modern-day humans," she went on. "In other words, into us." She walked over to her fork-tongued charge. "Not here, Artie," she warned, taking him by the hand as the kids made their way, joking and jostling, through the science museum.

Professor Xavier's students were just like normal teenagers on a field trip. But their appearance was a bit different from other kids'.

"But Miss Munroe, aren't we mutants?" Artie protested loudly, calling her by the name that all the students used.

Storm glanced around to make sure no one had heard him. Then she knelt down, tucking a piece of her white-blond hair behind her ear. "Yes, but mutants are only people with some extra-active genes," she reminded him. "We're still human."

Artie smiled at her. She smiled back and stood up. But when she turned to resume her lecture, she realized the rest of the students were gone. They had moved to the side and were staring at an exhibit on mutation.

Storm walked slowly over. Her stomach began to churn. The exhibit was filled with illustrations and photographs of hideously deformed mutants. A time line tracked mankind from the apelike *Homo habilis* to *Homo sapiens*. Then the line split into a second group, labeled HOMO_____? The kids looked confused, horrified, and hurt. It was more than she could bear.

"Come on, children," Storm said, her voice hardening. She put a reassuring arm around Artie's shoulders. "Let's go."

—X2—

Dr. Jean Grey smiled as she watched the students gather around the dinosaur display. They were so eager and smart, and they asked the most brilliant questions. As more visitors crowded into the museum, her smile faded. She tried to block out the mental whispers from the crowd, but soon the murmur had built into a chorus of voices that formed a cacophony in her mind. Jean grimaced and shut her eyes. It was overwhelming.

The glass wall behind her began to shake. Creaking and warping, it was almost ready to shatter when—

"Jean?"

Jean opened her eyes. The glass settled. The voices faded.

Scott Summers, known as Cyclops to the X-Men, was standing with a young girl. She held a sketchpad with a dinosaur on it.

"You okay?" he asked.

"Yeah. I'm fine," Jean said, swallowing. "It's just a headache." She could tell Cyclops wasn't convinced, but the girl was tugging on his sleeve, distracting him.

"You were talking about the extinction of the dinosaurs," the girl reminded him.

Cyclops pointed to a display. "I need to talk to Ms. Grey real quick. Can you draw me a picture of that big cat?"

The girl gave him a funny look. "It's a saber-toothed tiger."

Cyclops looked sheepish. "Right."

As the girl scampered off to do his bidding, Cyclops moved closer to Jean and touched her hand. She looked away. "It's not just a headache, is it?" he persisted.

She sighed, shaking her head.

He hesitated. "I wasn't sure how to say this, but ever since Liberty Island you've been—"

"Scott," Jean interrupted, not wanting to go there.

"—different," he finished.

Jean gazed around before allowing her eyes to settle back

on him. "My telepathy's been off lately," she said finally. "I can't seem to focus. I can hear . . . *everything*."

"A month ago you had to concentrate just to levitate a book across the room. Now when you're having nightmares, the entire bedroom shakes," Cyclops said worriedly. "It's not just your telepathy."

Jean stared across the room. For once, everything was silent. In her heart she knew Cyclops was right. "The dreams are getting worse," she confessed. "I keep feeling that something terrible is about to—" She broke off. "I—I don't want to lose you," she said quietly.

Cyclops threw his arms around her, hugging her tightly. "I'm not going anywhere."

Jean rested her head on his shoulder. His words and his presence were comforting, but still . . . still something was not right. She could feel it.

"Are we interrupting again?"

Jean and Cyclops looked up to see Storm, followed by her students. They smiled at one another.

"So . . . how was the giant squid?" Storm asked as she began to do a quick head count of the kids.

Jean laughed. "The kids liked it. Scott was bored."

"It was boring," Cyclops protested.

Jean was just about to launch into a defense of squid and their distant relatives when she caught the look of concern that had spread across Storm's face. "What is it?" she asked.

Storm was clearly flustered. "My count . . . where are the others?" she asked the students, who looked at one another, shrugging. She quickly did another count, and a distraught look took over her eyes.

Jean fought back worry and let the voices come into her mind. What she heard scared her. "We should find the professor," she told the others, not waiting for a response before she began the search.

—X2—

A flame hovered over a small lighter. *Poof!* The lighter snapped shut. The flame disappeared.

"I'll ask one more time," said the tall, gangly teen, his voice growing even angrier than it already had been.

John Allerdyce couldn't keep from grinning. His friends, Bobby Drake and Rogue, sat across from him. They looked very nervous.

"It's a simple question," said the gangly teen's shorter, uglier friend.

"And I'll give you a simple answer," John tossed back. He held on to the lighter.

The tall kid glowered at him. "Do. You. Have. A. Light?"

John pretended to think about the question. *Flick. Flick.*

15

Flick. The lighter went on and off again. "Sorry, pal. Can't help ya."

The kid clenched his fist.

"Knock it off, John," Rogue said quietly. She smoothed back the white streak in her long brown hair and gave him a pleading look.

"Please," Bobby added under his breath.

"Yeah, John," jeered the short kid. "Listen to your girl-friends."

John twirled his lighter and winked at Rogue. "I'm sorry, guys. Besides the fact that this is clearly marked as a non-smoking environment"—he pointed to a sign that stated the rule— "I couldn't bear knowing that I contributed to this young man's slow, tumor-ridden death."

Just as John flicked his lighter closed once more, the tall kid snatched it from his hand.

"What's this, a fashion accessory?" he sneered.

Now John was angry. These idiots didn't know who they were messing with. *Pyro.* He lunged for the lighter but the short kid got in his way, holding him down, stopping him from getting it. The tall kid lit his cigarette. He blew the smoke in Pyro's face.

Anger simmered and bubbled inside him as he stared at the glowing embers of the cigarette. He narrowed his eyes. The flame expanded.

And then the kid's jacket and hair and clothes were on fire.

"*Ahhh!* No!" the kid screamed, frantically trying to pat out the flames. His friend stood slack-jawed, in shock.

The entire food court crowd stood up, angling to see what was happening. Pyro smiled, flipping his long bangs from his eyes. Some people got exactly what was coming to them.

Fizzzt. Giving Pyro a reprimanding frown, Bobby sent a stream of frost toward the flaming kid, quickly snuffing the fire out. The kid dropped, crying, to the ground.

His friend stared down at him, horrified. Then he faced Pyro. He was just about to punch him when he froze. Literally.

Pyro looked around. Everyone in the food court except for him, Bobby, and Rogue, was completely motionless. A mother screaming at her kids . . . a man about to grope his girl-friend . . . an ice cream machine still running, overflowing a cone—the entire place was perfectly still.

Pyro bent down to grab his lighter. When he stood up, there was someone wheeling toward him. Professor Charles Xavier. And behind him were the school's teachers, Ms. Grey, Mr. Summers, Ms. Munroe, and the rest of the kids on the field trip.

Professor Xavier came into the food court, staring at Pyro and his friends with a look of anger and disappointment. Pyro looked down at his shoes. He knew he was wrong. But it was hard sometimes. Especially when he came face to face with such jerks.

A sound caught his attention, and he looked up at a TV mounted on a nearby wall.

An image of the White House surrounded by army troops flashed on the screen with the words *Mutant Assassination Attempt*.

Pyro watched as the adults shot one another horrified glances.

"Professor, I think it's time to go," urged Cyclops.

Xavier looked at the frozen crowd and then at the broadcast. "I think you're right."

Silently Pyro and his friends filed out of the museum, past all of the frozen people. Once the group was safely outside, these people would snap out of it and return to their normal lives, Pyro knew. He just wished he could be there to see what those two morons would do when they came back to life.

And to be honest, he wouldn't mind heating them up a bit again too.

CHAPTER THREE

THE X-MANSION

Cyclops had been pacing all afternoon. Now he stood in front of the staff lounge window, staring out at the grass, the gardens, the kids having a good time. Why did someone want to ruin this? "My opinion?" he said, turning around to face Jean, Storm, and Professor Xavier. "Magneto's behind this."

Jean shook her head. "No, I don't think so, Scott."

Xavier wheeled over. "While Eric might have organized something like this from prison, for him the gesture is far too . . . irrational. It only hurts his goal of mutant prosperity."

"You mean superiority," Cyclops corrected. Magneto was a powerful mutant who had given up on peaceful coexistence. He had already planned a terrorist strike against humankind. Attacking the president wasn't at all out of character.

"You're right. If Eric had his way," Xavier conceded, rubbing his bald head.

"You know how the government will respond to this," Storm said from her perch on a sofa. "They'll reintroduce the Registration Act."

"Or worse," Xavier muttered.

Cyclops frowned. Forcing mutants to expose themselves would mean their destruction. Nonmutants had treated mutants with hostility, fear—even violence. Mutants just wanted to live their lives like everybody else.

Jean's forehead creased. "Do you think the assassin was working alone?"

"The only way we'll know is if we find him before the authorities do." Professor X hesitated. "I've used Cerebro to track the mutant to Boston. Once I get more exact coordinates, Storm and Jean, I'll need you to take the X-Jet and try to pick him up."

Cyclops stared out the window once more, watching a pair of kids toss a ball back and forth. If only things could be as simple as a game of catch.

Back at the Oval Office, Stryker slowly rubbed the gouge on President McKenna's desk with his index finger. "It was close, wasn't it?" he said. "Closer than anyone's admitted."

The president poured two glasses of brandy. Stryker noticed that his hands were shaking slightly. "What do you need, William?"

"I need your authorization for a special operation," Stryker declared, flicking a minuscule fleck of dust from his custom-tailored pants.

The president sighed, then took a sip of his drink. "And somehow I thought you were here to talk about school reform."

Stryker gave him a sly smile. "Funny you should say that."

The door opened and an assistant let Senator Kelly in.

"Senator," said the president.

"Mr. President," said Kelly as they shook hands. "Thanks for having me."

"I don't believe you two have met," President McKenna said, walking Kelly over to Stryker. "Senator Kelly, this is William Stryker. His department has been dealing with the mutant phenomenon since before my time."

Stryker rubbed his stubbled chin. "As I recall, you were a staunch supporter of the Registration Act, Senator, but it seems your ideas on the mutant problem have changed recently."

Senator Kelly smiled. "For the best, I hope."

"I thought the senator's point of view would be worthwhile, particularly during this crisis," President McKenna explained.

Stryker tried to look deferential. "If you think that's appropriate."

"So, what are you proposing, Mr. Stryker?" the senator asked him.

Stryker had no choice. The president valued the senator's opinion. So Stryker would have to look like he did as well. He began placing surveillance photos of the mansion of Charles Xavier onto the president's desk. "We've managed to gather evidence of a mutant training facility in the Salem region of upstate New York," he said matter-of-factly.

"Where did you get this information?" the president asked him, perusing one of the photos.

"Interrogation of one of the mutant terrorists from the Liberty Island Incident."

"Eric? Eric Lensherr?" Senator Kelly asked incredulously. "You have access to him?"

Stryker continued to put photographs on the desk. "My group developed the technology that built his plastic prison. But it appears I'm not the only one with access to him." He threw down the next photo with extra emphasis. "This is Charles Xavier, leader of this training faculty, and a longtime associate of Mr. Lensherr. Apparently Xavier has friends in the Justice Department and has paid Lensherr several visits."

Stryker proceeded with more photographs and files. Kelly looked at them suspiciously. "This facility is a school," he pointed out, frowning.

"Sure it is," Stryker said, throwing down another photograph. *This one has a brain,* he thought, mildly irritated by the notion.

"What's that?" the president asked, peering at a photograph of the basketball court. Next to it was a gigantic sleek-looking aircraft.

"It's a jet," Stryker said. *Obviously.*

"What kind of jet?" the president asked.

"We don't know," Stryker said, trying not to sound as if he were talking to a five-year-old, though he felt as if he were. "But it comes up out of the basketball court." He waited a moment, then sadly shook his head. "If we'd been allowed to do our jobs before this incident . . ."

The president held up a hand, signifying that he'd heard enough.

Stryker was pleased to see that Senator Kelly looked sufficiently nervous.

"Listen, William," the president said to him. "You enter. You detain. You question. But the last thing I want to hear is that we've spilled the blood of an innocent mutant child. You understand?"

Stryker held up his palms. "Hey . . . only if they shoot first, Mr. President."

A few moments later, Stryker strode out of the office into the reception area. As he knew she would be, Yuriko Oyama was waiting for him. Tall and beautiful, with glossy dark hair swept off to the side and pale blue eyes, she nodded at him and joined him as he walked down the hallway. Workmen were patching up the walls and replacing torn carpet. *That attack must really have been something,* Stryker thought, taking it in.

"Mr. Stryker?"

He turned. Senator Kelly jogged down the corridor toward him.

"Oh. Senator Kelly, this is Yuriko, my personal assass—assistant," Stryker said.

Yuriko clasped Kelly's hand and shook it hard.

"That's quite a handshake," the senator said, pulling back after a few seconds.

As the three of them walked down the hall, Stryker cast a wary glance at the senator. "What can I do for you?"

"Eric Lensherr's prison," the senator said. "I'd like to arrange a visit, if possible."

Stryker raised an eyebrow. "It isn't a petting zoo, Senator. In this conflict he is the enemy and you're just a spectator." He smiled. "So why don't you just sit this one out, all right?"

Senator Kelly didn't look like he was going to listen. "Are you trying to turn this into some kind of war?"

"I was piloting Black-Ops missions into the jungles of North Vietnam while your mother was changing your diapers at Woodstock, Kelly. Don't talk to me about war," Stryker snapped as the senator halted his steps. "This already *is* a war."

Stryker and Yuriko walked on. If Stryker had turned around, he would have seen something very disturbing: Senator Kelly, rubbing his fingers together . . . and his eyes flashing an eerie, murky yellow.

CHAPTER FOUR

MAGNETO'S PLASTIC PRISON

A thin beam of light shone down on Magneto as he turned the pages of his book, T. H. White's *The Once and Future King*. Reading was always a pleasurable activity. If only he weren't in this detestable plastic prison. Plastic chairs. Plastic walls. Plastic chess pawns. He wouldn't have been surprised if they'd given him a plastic book to read and plastic food to eat.

He looked up to see the clear Plexiglas door open and his guard, the obnoxious Mitchell Laurio, step in from the long Habitrail-like entryway tube.

"Mr. Laurio," Magneto said wearily, wondering if he was about to go through another round of torture at the guard's beefy hands. "How long can we keep this up?"

"How long is your sentence?" Laurio barked, his shoes squeaking on the plastic floor.

Magneto smiled slightly. His ability to manipulate metal and create magnetic fields was useless as long as he was confined here. "Forever." He heard the slight click of the cameras in the prison shutting off. He swallowed. It was always bad when the cameras went off. The evil ones only did that when they didn't want evidence of their brutality on tape.

"Not necessarily forever, Mr. Lensherr," came an oily voice over the loudspeaker. "Just until I've got all that I need." Seconds later William Stryker came strutting in as if he owned the place. Round glasses emphasized the beadiness of his eyes, and his mustache twitched with impatience.

"Mr. Stryker," Magneto greeted the corrupt politician. "How kind of you to visit. Have you come back to make sure the taxpayers' dollars are keeping me . . . comfortable?"

Stryker didn't answer him. Instead, he sat down at the table across from him. He took out a small pipette of yellow liquid that Magneto recognized all too well.

Fear began pulsing through Magneto's body. He couldn't let Stryker inject him with that. For that would mean—

He tried to stand up, but Laurio roughly forced him back down, pressing his face to the table. He thought he heard Stryker laugh.

Magneto tried to resist as Laurio bent his head down. "No!" he cried, twisting in his seat. But he was no match for his burly assailant. Stryker leaned over and put two drops of the yellow liquid on the back of his neck, directly on the small circular scar that sat there.

For a second, Magneto thought he could gather his emotions and fight back. But those thoughts sailed out of his brain and were replaced by a sudden calm. Nothingness.

The liquid bubbled and sank into his neck, forming a perfect circle. His eyes widened. He was numb. Spineless. Brainless.

"Now, Mr. Lensherr," Stryker began, flexing his fingers as Magneto stared back at him, dazed. "I'd like to have one final talk about the house that Xavier built . . . and the machine called Cerebro."

—X2—

It was a good thing everyone was paying attention to the TV, Rogue decided as she and Bobby continued their thumb-wrestling match in the X-Mansion's TV room. Because if they hadn't been, someone might have noticed that Bobby had stopped trying to win and was moving closer to her on the couch.

Rogue swallowed. She liked Bobby so much. First off, he was undeniably cute, with his short, spiky light brown hair, soulful eyes, and soft red lips. And he was nice, too. Nice and sweet and smart—all the things a girl could want. But romance was pretty complicated with someone like her.

Someone who could absorb all of another person's energy with a single touch. Yeah, dating was a bit rough.

She looked up at Bobby as he moved closer to her. Was he going to risk kissing her?

Suddenly the sound of a roaring motorcycle filled the mansion. Kids looked up, questioning. But Rogue didn't. She gave Bobby a quick smile, then got up and ran to the foyer.

"Logan!" she cried as her friend stepped through the carved mahogany doorway. He looked just as she had remembered, his weathered face scruffy with stubble, his dark thick hair gelled back messily, a self-assured smile on his lips.

"Miss me, kid?" he teased.

"Not really." Then she giggled and threw her arms around him. He hugged her back, then pulled away.

"Who's this?" he asked.

Rogue turned to see Bobby behind her. She flushed. "This is Bobby, he's—"

"Her boyfriend," Bobby said firmly.

Rogue stared at him. Bobby actually seemed jealous! She watched as he and Logan shook hands. Crackling ice and vapors rose from their handshake. Rogue rolled her eyes. Bobby could keep that from happening if he wanted to. He was just showing off.

"They call me Iceman," Bobby said, puffing out his chest slightly.

Logan cocked an eyebrow. "Right. Boyfriend. . . . How do you guys—"

"We're working on that," Bobby said quickly.

Rogue looked away. Sometimes her mutant power could really be embarrassing.

"So where's the professor?" Logan asked them.

"Look who's come back!" Storm came jogging down the steps. "And just in time," she added.

"For what?" Logan asked.

"We need a baby-sitter," said Storm, kissing him lightly on the cheek.

"Baby-sitter?"

Rogue watched as Storm pulled back and gave Logan a glimpse of Dr. Grey, who was on the staircase. Logan could try to act all cool, but Rogue could tell he was nervous to see her again.

"Hi, Logan," Dr. Grey said, her face slightly flushed at the unexpected visitor. Her green eyes were warm.

"Hey, Jean."

Seeing your teacher flirt was pretty interesting, Rogue decided. She watched as Dr. Grey smiled up at Logan. "It's good to have you home," she told him.

"How good?"

Storm began backing up slowly. "I'm—I'm gonna get the jet ready." She pointed toward the door, then gave Bobby and Rogue a conspiratorial smile. "Bye!"

Bobby began pulling Rogue back toward the lounge. She

wanted to shrug him off, but she was pretty sure the adults wanted to be alone. "Bye, Logan," Rogue said, reluctant to say bye so soon after hello.

Logan gave her a grin. "See you later."

"Nice to meet you," Bobby called as they headed back to their perch on the sofa. *Wonder what Bobby meant by "working on it"?* Rogue thought, feeling slightly breathless.

Maybe getting pulled away from Logan and Ms. Grey wasn't so bad after all.

— X2 —

Logan gave Jean an appraising glance. "You look good," he told her, his mouth curling into a smile. Her hair was shorter now, with a cute little flip. She was everything he had remembered—and better.

She smiled back. "So do you." She looked as if she was going to say something else, but then stopped and cleared her throat. "Storm and I are heading to Boston. The professor wants us to track a mutant who attacked the president. We won't be gone long."

Logan could feel the smile slipping from his face. "But I just got here," he protested.

"And you'll be here when we get back again," she said. Then she crossed her arms. "Unless you plan on running off again."

There was so much he wanted to tell her. But he needed

time . . . and he didn't want to be in the middle of a school when he did it. "I can probably think of a few reasons to stick around," he said at last.

"Find what you were looking for, Logan?" came Cyclops's voice from upstairs.

Jean turned as Scott came down the stairs. But Logan's eyes never left Jean's face. "More or less," he said.

He could tell she was nervous, that she didn't quite trust what might happen between him and Cyclops.

But I'm back, thought Logan. *She's going to have to deal with it. With me.*

"I'll see you boys later," Jean said, giving them a small wave.

"Be safe, okay?" Cyclops told her as she leaned over and gave him a kiss.

"You too," she said as she pulled away and looked at Logan.

"See ya," Logan called to her as she left the room. He tossed Scott the keys to his motorcycle. "Your bike needs gas."

Cyclops threw the keys hard back to Logan. "Then fill her up." He stalked off.

Logan watched him go. He didn't want an enemy. But getting what he really wanted might just get him one.

—X2—

Professor X sat in his wheelchair in front of Cerebro's console in the X-Mansion. He didn't look up. "Logan, my repeated requests about smoking in the mansion notwithstanding, continue smoking *that* in *here* and you will spend the rest of your days under the belief that you are a six-year-old girl."

Logan wagged his cigar at him. "You'd do that?"

Xavier raised an eyebrow. "I'll have Jean braid your hair."

Not wanting to call the professor's bluff, Logan put out the cigar on his palm and stuck it in his shirt pocket for later. He stepped farther into the huge spherical chamber and walked down the platform toward Professor X. The door behind him closed with a heavy click.

Xavier put on his helmet and Cerebro hummed to life.

Logan looked around, remembering his first time in here. Professor X had waited for him to leave the room before starting things up. He wasn't sure he should be there now. "You want me to leave?" he asked, uncertain.

Xavier shook his head slightly. "No. Just . . . don't move."

Professor X sat completely still as Cerebro buzzed and quivered. Then the glistening metal walls fell away. Logan felt an incredible rush of speed, as if he were bolting through an endless blackness with hints of light. His stomach lurched. In seconds, he and Xavier were in a deep black void. A giant image of Earth rotated above them. Dotted across the continents were sparkling white and red lights. They reminded Logan of fallen stars. There were a lot more white stars than red ones.

"These lights represent every living person on the planet," Xavier explained. "The white lights are humans."

Suddenly the white lights faded, leaving only the red ones. There weren't as many as the white, but there were a lot. "You see," the professor went on, "we're not as alone as you think."

"I found the base at Alkali Lake," Logan told him. "There was nothing there."

But Xavier didn't answer. He was focusing on the lights, which had completely faded now. All that was left was a red line trailing along the eastern coast of the United States.

"This broken line represents the path of the mutant who attacked the president," Xavier said, thinking aloud. "I'm finding it hard to lock on to him."

"Can't you just concentrate harder?" Logan asked. Seemed easy enough.

"If I wanted to kill him, yes."

Cerebro zoomed in closer, revealing a blinking red light in what Logan thought had to be Boston.

"It looks like he's finally stopped running," Xavier said. "There." Having found what he needed, he closed his eyes.

Whoosh! The Cerebro effect collapsed on itself. Logan blinked, and he was back on the catwalk. He frowned. "Look. I need you to read my mind again."

"I'm afraid the results will be the same as before," Xavier said.

Logan crossed his arms, fighting to keep his control. "We had a deal." That was why he had come back in the first place. That, and Jean Grey, if he had to admit it.

Xavier let out a breath. "Logan, the mind is not a box to be simply unlocked and opened. It's a beehive with a million separate compartments." He gave a small shrug. "I don't doubt that your amnesia and skeletal enhancements are connected, but . . ." He drifted off.

Logan didn't want to hear his excuses. He wanted help.

Xavier put his helmet down. "Logan, sometimes there are things the mind needs to discover for itself."

If Xavier thought he was going to be disappointed, he was wrong. Logan was mad.

"I promise we'll talk more when I return," Xavier said, bringing the discussion to a close. "If you'd be so kind to watch over the children tonight, Scott and I are going to pay an old friend a visit."

Xavier wheeled himself out, leaving Logan standing there. So he was reduced to being a baby-sitter, was that it?

He sighed. There were worse things.

CHAPTER FIVE

NEW YORK AIRSPACE

The X-Jet soared through the clouds over Westchester, New York.

"Yes, Professor," Storm said into the cockpit radio, leaving Jean to man the controls. "Go ahead."

"I'm sending the mutant's coordinates to you now. Once you land, you'll have to rely on your skills to track him."

"Let's hope he cooperates," Storm said as the black jet raced faster.

"Yes, for his sake. Good luck," Professor X told her before cutting out.

Storm's fingers gripped the armrest. The plane was going incredibly fast. She stared at the controls as the roar of the engine peaked.

BOOM!

"Jean!" Storm cried, realizing that her friend was in a complete daze. They'd just broken the sound barrier!

Jean jolted upright, as if she'd just been caught napping. "S-sorry," she stammered, looking helplessly at the blinking lights and gears in front of her.

Storm grabbed hold of the controls and slowed down the jet. Once they were back to a safe flying speed, she looked over at her friend.

"What's wrong?" she asked worriedly. This lapse of focus wasn't like the normally single-minded Jean.

"Nothing," Jean insisted, hastily smoothing back her glossy red hair. "I'm just feeling a little off."

"A little?" Storm wasn't buying it. "Maybe it's just that Logan's back in town," she joked, trying to lighten the mood.

"Maybe it is," Jean said softly.

Storm's smile faded. She'd only been kidding. But Jean wasn't.

—X2—

Yuriko Oyama entered the lobby of the federal building, walking against the streaming foot traffic of eager employees heading home for the day. She strode past a cleaning crew and pressed her palm against a hand scanner. As expected, the door unlocked.

She shut the door and walked past a glass panel into William Stryker's office. Her body began to shift and a smile darted between the corners of her mouth. She had transformed back into her true self. Mystique, a shape-shifter who did what Magneto told her to.

She slid in front of a computer and turned it on.

"Voiceprint Identification please," came the computer's monotone question.

"Stryker, William," Mystique said, replicating the man's oily inflection perfectly. She could imitate anybody, right down to his voice.

ACCESS GRANTED flashed across the monitor.

She selected Recent Items from a menu and found a folder marked Lensherr. Inside was a series of files: a mug shot and profile of Magneto, layouts of the plastic prison, and a bunch of employee photos.

Mystique chose one of Mitchell Laurio, smiled, and hit a computer key. The printer next to her hummed to life.

As the files printed, Mystique's eyes wandered to another electronic folder, one labeled 143. Curious, she opened it.

Classified surveillance photos of Xavier's mansion, files about the mutant Nightcrawler, diagrams of Cerebro, and a map showing the layout of a massive base flashed onto the screen. Mystique scowled, then pressed Print again.

The last page was coming through the printer when Mystique heard a noise in the hallway.

Now the real Yuriko Oyama entered the office and headed

for the desk. She unlocked a drawer with a set of keys and pulled out some files, an ID badge, and sunglasses, tossing everything into a briefcase.

Mystique moved slightly and Yuriko whipped around. "What are you doing in here?" she snapped to the meek-looking janitor who was gazing helplessly at her.

"Lo siento, la puerta estaba abierta." The janitor who was Mystique apologized profusely, backing out of the room with a wastebasket that was full of freshly printed files. Being a shape-shifter definitely had its good points.

Mystique quickly began walking down the hallway, still in the guise of the janitor, and still toting a wastebasket filled with printouts. She barely noticed the real janitor, his mouth agape as she passed him.

—X2—

The X-Jet had landed quietly in Boston Harbor. Now it lay hidden under the surface of the cool New England water, empty of its crew.

Jean's shaky telekinesis had left her feeling wobbly and fragile. She was glad Storm was with her as they walked cautiously down the cobbled brick street and into the abandoned church. They wore trench coats over their black leather uniforms, blending seamlessly into the night.

"These are the coordinates," Jean said as a gust of wind rattled the door behind them. They walked inside, taking note of some antimutant graffiti on a nearby wall. Jean could feel Storm tense angrily beside her as she read the words. Thunder rumbled from above.

"They'll never let us live our lives," Storm hissed angrily.

The two friends walked down the aisle. At the base of the altar sat a lone lit candle, its flame flickering as if blown by a gentle breeze. An open Bible was placed next to it.

"Gehen sie raus . . . ," came a whispered voice.

Jean listened attentively as the voice grew stronger, trying to place its source. Was it coming from the balcony? *"Ich bin ein Bote des Teufels!"*

"We're not here to hurt you," Storm called out, searching for the voice's owner. "We just want to talk."

A dark figure climbed in the rafters above them. *"Ich bin die Ausgeburt des Bosen!"* he called out.

"He's a teleporter," Jean realized aloud. "Must be why the professor had trouble locking on to him."

"Ich bin ein Daemon!" the voice shouted, growing louder.

Jean rolled her eyes. This was so childish. "Are you bored yet?" she asked Storm.

Storm snorted. "Oh yeah." Her face was a mask of concentration. Lightning twisted and coiled up the church's columns, striking a rafter. The dark figure plummeted.

Bamf! He disappeared in a cloud of smoke.

Jean held up a hand, and *bamf!* he was there again, this time frozen in midair, held by Jean's own mutant power.

"You have him?" Storm asked her as the creature futilely kicked and squirmed.

"He's not going anywhere," Jean said firmly, watching as he tried to teleport. All he got for his efforts were some weak puffs of smoke. "Are you?" she said to him.

"Please don't kill me," he babbled in German-accented English, his eyes nervous and quick. Jean could see vague wrinkles in his blue skin. "I never intended to harm anyone!"

Storm didn't look entirely convinced. "I wonder how people got that impression." She eyed him. "What's your name?"

Now it was his turn to eyeball them. "Kurt . . . Kurt Wagner," he said. And for some reason, Jean believed him.

—X2—

"You'll be fine," Jean assured him as she tended to the bullet wound near his shoulder. Kurt, known also as Nightcrawler, had taken them into the small room that was his home inside the church's tall spiral tower. Well-thumbed Bibles and hymnals lay scattered about next to blankets and some cans of food. Old, curling circus posters with pictures of Kurt and the words "The Incredible Nightcrawler" hung from the walls. "The worst you'll have is a scar," Jean said.

Nightcrawler clutched the rosary he held in his hands even tighter, wincing as she wrapped a bandage around his arm.

"What about these?" Storm asked, pointing to a series of tattooed symbols that covered his dark blue face and body. "Did you do them yourself?"

"Yes," Nightcrawler whispered, his pointy blue ears twitching.

Jean finished dressing the wound and watched as Nightcrawler put his shirt back on. He had been telling them about the attack he'd made on the White House, but he seemed confused and uncertain. "You were saying?" she prompted, steering the conversation back.

Nightcrawler swallowed. "I could see it all happening," he said, his blue face agitated. "But I couldn't help myself. It was like a bad dream."

"And before you were in the White House, what do you remember?" Storm asked.

He looked anxiously at them. "Nothing."

Storm sighed. "Jean?"

Dr. Grey didn't know what to make of him. But it wasn't good. "I'd rather get him back to the professor," she told Storm. Then she noticed something on Nightcrawler's neck. "And what about this?" she asked, pointing.

It was a small, circular scar.

CHAPTER SIX

THE X-MANSION

No. No. He couldn't take the pain much longer. They were stab-bing his naked skin, gouging it, using—what were they using? Picks? Forks? Scalpels? Cold, pointy things that hurt. They thought he was sleeping, but he wasn't. Was he? His eyes flickered hazily. He was in a room. There wasn't much light. A tank of yel-low liquid sat on the floor. They were holding him, keeping him down, not letting him move. He had to go. Had to get out of there. A woman in a lab coat gripped a large syringe. She would use it on him if he didn't— Aargh! He was up; he was moving. Metal wrist cuffs went flying. Metal claws shot out in defense. And then he was out, running for his life through a snowy forest, the banks of a river not that far away—

"Unh!" Logan's eyes slammed open as he bolted upright,

beads of sweat dotting his upper lip. It was the dream again, he told himself, trying to slow the rapid beating of his heart. It was always that stupid, torturous dream.

Tossing the tangled bedsheets aside, Logan stood up, running a hand through his coarse dark hair. He wandered out into the quiet hall of the X-Mansion. Music, then muted laughter, came from the TV room. Logan walked to the doorway. On the couch sat a kid Logan knew was called Jones. Logan moved behind the couch, watching as the TV changed channels. Cooking programs, late-night talk shows, cartoons, movies all flashed before his eyes. Logan turned his gaze toward Jones. The boy wasn't using a remote control. Whenever he blinked, the channel changed.

Logan chuckled.

Jones looked up, blinking. "Can't sleep?"

"How can you tell?"

Jones turned back to the TV. " 'Cause you're awake."

Great conversation they were having. "Right. How about you?"

"I don't sleep," Jones said flatly.

"Right," Logan said as a news channel came on. "You guys got any beer?"

"Try the kitchen."

Thanks for being so helpful, Logan thought as he walked down the hallway and into the kitchen. He had company. Rogue's friend Bobby was sitting at a small table, eating a bowl of ice cream. Ignoring him, Logan opened up the fridge and peered inside. Milk, OJ, butter, some leftover casserole-looking thing—but no beer.

Bobby's voice startled him. "Hi."

"Hey," Logan said, shutting the door. "Got any beer?"

Bobby gave him a strange look. "This is a school."

Logan sighed. "So that's a no?" He opened a cabinet and found a six-pack—of soda. Resignedly pulling one out, he walked over and sat down across from Bobby. Then he tapped his fingers on the table. So this was the guy Rogue was with. He pulled a bottle from the pack.

"They're warm," Logan groaned, as if this was exactly what he'd expected on a no-beer baby-sitting night.

Bobby reached over and grabbed Logan's bottle. Ice crackled. Mist appeared in the air. Logan looked down at his newly frost-covered soda.

"Not anymore," Bobby said, pleased.

Logan nodded, impressed. "Handy."

Bobby smiled and helped himself to a bottle. Logan smiled too. If Bobby meant something to Rogue, then Logan might as well get to know him a little better.

Three guards stood watch outside Magneto's plastic prison as Professor X and Cyclops entered the security area.

"I'll take it from here," said one of the guards, stepping toward them. A tiny tag that read LAURIO was pinned to his pale gray security uniform.

Not one to back down, Cyclops stared at the guard through his visor.

"It's all right, Scott," said Professor X. He smiled encouragingly at him. Cyclops stepped away, letting Laurio push the professor's special plastic wheelchair toward the metal detection area.

"Nice shades." Laurio sneered at Cyclops.

Cyclops looked straight ahead. "Thanks."

Professor X let his hands rest on the plastic arms as he nodded good-bye to Cyclops. Laurio wheeled him down the plastic entryway tube and into Magneto's cell. It had been some time since he'd seen the face of his old friend . . . a friend whose beliefs had turned him into a lethal nemesis.

Magneto's back was turned, but a slight movement told the professor that his presence was felt. "Charles Xavier," Magneto said, a hint of mocking in his voice. "Have you come to rescue me?"

"Sorry, Eric," Professor X said sadly. "Not today."

"To what do I owe the pleasure?"

"The assassination attempt on the president." Professor

X let his words linger for a moment. "What do you know about it?"

"Nothing," said Magneto. "Just what I read in the papers. You shouldn't even have to ask." Magneto turned to face him, and Xavier was shocked to see bruises peppering his face.

"What's happened to you?" asked the professor. Despite every terrible thing Magneto had masterminded, Xavier was concerned. After all, they had a history together. Eric Lensherr had helped him understand what he was, helped him learn how to use his powers.

"I've had frequent visits from William Stryker." Magneto's icy eyes clouded over. "You remember him, don't you?"

Professor X thought for a moment. "William Stryker," he repeated. "I haven't heard that name in years."

"His son Jason was once a student of yours, wasn't he?" Magneto prompted.

Xavier nodded slowly, remembering the mutant child. "Yes. Unfortunately, I wasn't able to help him. At least, not the way his father wanted me to."

"And now you think that taking in the Wolverine will make up for your failure with Stryker's son," Magneto surmised, stroking his chin.

The professor was silent.

"You haven't told him about his past, have you?" Magneto asked him.

"I've put him on the path, but Logan's mind is still fragile," Professor X said staunchly.

"Is it?" Magneto asked. "Or are you afraid you'll lose one of your precious X-Men?" He sighed deeply and turned away.

Professor X had no other recourse. He focused, concentrating on reading Magneto's mind. As he began to absorb his former friend's thoughts, his face twisted in horror. "Eric," he got out with a gasp. "What have you done?"

There was a moment of silence. "I'm sorry, Charles," Magneto said, a glimmer of true regret in his eyes. "I—I couldn't help it."

"What have you told Stryker?" the professor asked, dreading the answer that he felt would come.

Magneto averted his gaze. "Everything."

Xavier pushed back hard in his chair, horrified. That meant—that meant— He tried not to despair as a cacophony of thoughts filled his brain. He was deep into sorting them out when a slight hiss caught his attention. He looked up at the small holes that lined the cell's wall. Gas was streaming in.

"Scott!" Professor X yelled, waving his arms. The air was getting thicker. Coughing, he fell from his wheelchair onto the floor.

Magneto dropped to his knees, choking. He looked over at Xavier, his eyes full of remorse. "You should have killed me, Charles," he croaked out weakly. "When you had the chance."

The two men struggled for air. And then they passed out.

Cyclops was watching through the glass window as Professor X screamed. "What the hell is going on?" he yelled at the guards as *thwap!* a small dart slammed into his back. It jolted him, but it wasn't able to penetrate his leather uniform. He spun around to see a tall Asian woman holding a dart pistol.

Fury filled him as he fired an optic blast, hitting the woman and destroying the gun in a single burst. She slammed hard into the wall, causing a large gash in her head. A trickle of blood slid down her cheek.

Cyclops braced himself as the guards rushed him. He was able to aim and blast one of them, but Laurio managed to pull his hand away from his red crystal visor. Cyclops snatched a nightstick from the other guard and swung it hard into Laurio's stomach. The man thudded to the floor. *Wham!* Cyclops smashed the club into the other guard's face.

Across the room the woman got up and leaped toward him, flinging him into the door. Cyclops had time only to realize that the large wound on her head was gone. *It healed itself. Just like Logan,* he thought dizzily. And then in one fluid motion the woman launched backward and twisted, kicking him across the face and knocking him unconscious to the ground in a crushing blow.

Helicopters silently dropped and landed in the X-Mansion's giant backyard. Soldiers crept quietly through the mansion grounds. They had cut the external electrical wires. There was no power. No telephone. No way to escape.

Now all they needed were the kids.

CHAPTER SEVEN

THE X-MANSION—
later that night

Jones sat alone on the couch, laughing softly at an old *I Love Lucy* episode. *Blink.* The channel changed to an infomercial. *Blink.* Now one of those lame dating shows. Except that as he watched the couple on TV, the reflection of another person— a person there in the room with him—appeared on the screen.

He turned around to see a man dressed in black battle gear. His face was completely covered by a military mask, goggles over his eyes. He waved to Jones.

Weird. What was going on? Was the school having some sort of drill? Jones got off the couch and walked toward him. "Hi."

The man pulled out a pistol and fired it directly at Jones's head. *Bang!* Jones fell to the floor, a dart stuck in his neck. His eyes fluttered and the TV changed channels behind him as the man motioned to a legion of other soldiers. They flooded into the mansion, rushing up both staircases and into the upstairs hallway. Two by two, they began entering the students' rooms.

---X2---

"My parents think this is a prep school," Bobby admitted, absently stirring what was left of his melted strawberry ice cream.

Logan shrugged. That was the story Professor X gave to the world in order to help mutant kids learn to focus their powers and avoid persecution. "Hey, lots of prep schools have their own campus, dorms, and—"

"Jets?" Bobby finished wryly for him.

Logan leaned back in his chair, sizing Bobby up. "So . . . you and Rogue, huh?"

Bobby looked perplexed. "What? Oh, yeah . . . it's not what you think, though. I mean, I'd like it to be—" He stopped, flustered by the stern look Logan was giving him.

"It's just that it's not easy," he backpedaled. "When you want to be closer to someone but you can't be."

Logan knew exactly what the kid meant. And how he felt. Seeing Dr. Grey again—

Suddenly a faint noise echoed from the hall. Logan and Bobby looked up, alarmed. Logan motioned for him to be quiet, then snuck out the kitchen's back door.

The first bedroom was dark and still as the soldiers crept inside, their weapons raised. Two girls lay sleeping peacefully in their beds. One of the soldiers pointed his dart gun at the first girl, then fired. It was a perfectly aimed shot. But the bullet didn't hit her. Because the girl, Kitty Pryde, phased through the bed and through the hardwood floor, and landed next to a couch on the level below.

Alone in the kitchen, Bobby was getting nervous. He was so busy looking in front of him that he didn't notice the soldier who was silently creeping up behind him, aiming a dart gun at his unsuspecting neck.

The soldier didn't get very far.

"Ugh . . . ," the soldier squeaked out as the air was squeezed from his lungs. The gun fell from his grasp. "You picked the wrong house, bub," Logan hissed, not loosening his choke hold for a second, as Bobby stumbled back in shock.

—X2—

The soldier was just about to fire the gun into the remaining sleeping girl in the room, Siryn, when her eyes snapped open. She took a large breath and screamed a scream that made the mirror shatter and the soldier drop his gun so he could cover his ears, crying from the pain.

Thwap! A dart from the pistol of a soldier standing on the outside grounds stuck in Siryn's neck. Another soldier was moving forward to grab her when a huge shadow fell over the room. In the doorway stood another mutant student, Colossus. In his powerful arms were two unconscious soldiers. He flung them aside and stepped into the room. Organic-looking armor formed in plates around his chest and arms.

The terrified soldiers fired dozens of rounds at him.

But the bullets slid off him like mercury.

Scooping up Siryn, Colossus smashed down a wall. Then, with his friend in his arms, he stepped into the hallway.

—X2—

The entire X-Mansion had been rocked by Siryn's cry. Students woke up instantly, clutching their ears. Pyro windmilled, flailing, and fell out of bed. Rogue's eyes snapped open.

Logan jolted at the sound, giving the soldier in his grasp a chance to wrench free and pull out a rifle.

Alarmed, Bobby dove behind a counter. The soldier fired off a round. Then Logan knocked the gun away.

"Yeah?" the soldier yelled, pulling out a large knife. He lunged at Logan.

Logan grabbed the soldier's wrist, trying to push the knife away. *Slash*. The blade cut a gash in his cheek.

Snikt! Logan's claws popped out. Wide-eyed, the soldier stared, transfixed with fear. The two men struggled for the upper hand. Logan's claws went closer—and his wound began to heal. Then his claws pierced the soldier's flesh.

Snikt! The claws retracted. The soldier lay slumped on the floor.

And Logan and Bobby were running down the hall to fight whoever had invaded their home.

—X2—

Bobby didn't want to do anything that would upset Logan. After all, he'd just witnessed the guy give someone a total body piercing with his claws. But he couldn't stay put in the alcove Logan had stuck him in while the kids above him screamed in fear.

Taking a quick look around him, he darted across the hall and into the X-Mansion elevator.

It was chaos on the next floor. Helicopters rumbled outside, their spotlights shining into the windows. Screaming kids ran from their rooms.

Bobby spotted Pyro, coughing and looking completely panicked. "John, where's Rogue?" he asked, grabbing his shoulders.

Pyro shook his head. "I don't know."

"I'm going to find her," Bobby said, taking off. Seconds later he felt Pyro running by his side.

—X2—

Jones was surprisingly heavy, Logan thought as he carried the boy down the carpeted hallway. He'd come across some soldiers trying to lift the kid up. Those soldiers weren't going to be doing much of anything now. Logan had sliced them and stabbed them and yanked out the darts they'd fired into him—and the dart that was lodged in Jones's neck.

"You're alive," Logan whispered as Jones mumbled and moaned, slipping in and out of consciousness. He hoped he could say the same for Bobby. The Iceman hadn't waited for him in the alcove. Logan didn't blame him—but that meant one more person he had to find.

At the far end of the corridor he spotted Colossus shepherding a group of frightened kids into a secret wall passage.

"Hey, Shorty!" Logan yelled. When he reached him, Logan handed over Jones into Colossus's massive hands.

"But I can help you!" Colossus blurted out, the weight of Jones's body like a feather in his arms.

Logan nodded to the kids who had fled into the passage. "Help them."

It was a game of cat and mouse. Logan pressed his back against the wall as two flashlights approached from down the hallway. And then he spun around the corner.

The light from the flashlights stumbled and shook—and one fell on the floor. Logan didn't stop to wonder why. He had kids to save.

—X2—

Rogue raced down the X-Mansion corridor with a girl she recognized from the TV room. Rogue's hair was a tangled mess, and she wished she'd stopped to grab a bathrobe to put over her skimpy nightgown. As the two ran, they stumbled across a little girl crouched in a doorway, crying softly. Rogue went to her, imagining how frightened and cold she must feel. "Come on, honey," she urged gently, motioning for her to follow.

Sniffling, the girl got up and joined them. When they reached the end of the corridor, Rogue pressed her hand against a section of the wall near a large bay window. A small door slid open, revealing a hidden passageway. Quickly she ushered the girls inside.

"Aren't you coming?" asked the older girl.

"I have to find someone first," Rogue said hurriedly. "When you come out of the tunnels, run straight to the first house you can find—tell them you ran away from home. And whatever you do, don't tell them you're a mutant. Okay?"

The younger girl paused, clearly frightened. Rogue lifted a wisp of hair from her face and smiled. "Okay," she agreed, ducking inside.

Rogue shut the door, turned, and ran back down to the end of the hallway. Through the noise of helicopters and screams, she heard a distant voice.

"Rogue!"

Bobby and Pyro rounded a corner at the far end of the hall. They ran to meet her.

"This way!" she shouted, practically bursting with relief to see that Bobby was okay. Just as she turned to lead them toward the secret passage, a helicopter spotlight filled the bay window, silhouetting two soldiers. They were dangling in front of the window, attaching small grenades to the edges.

Rogue gasped as Bobby pulled her and Pyro back around the corner to safety.

Smash! The window exploded, sending glass and wood everywhere. Rogue listened as the soldiers swung through the debris and landed. And then she ran.

When they reached the bottom of the stairs, Rogue pulled back in fear. Two soldiers lay on the floor, motionless. Were they dead? She didn't have time to find out because four more soldiers burst through the front door, their guns raised.

Rogue froze, gulping down the fear that threatened to choke her. They were trapped. She shot Bobby a panicked look as the soldiers aimed green lasers at their chests.

"Rarrrrrr!" Rogue and her friends looked up to see Logan leap off the balcony, his claws bared and arms spread wide. *Slash!* He stabbed his claws through the shoulders of two soldiers, pinning them to the floor. Before the other two could even fire, Logan jammed his claws into their legs, flipping them onto their backs.

Blood spattered on his gray tank top. "Let's go!" he told the teenagers.

A helicopter spotlight shone through the front door. Rogue could hear the sounds of more soldiers approaching. Following Logan's lead, they turned and ran back inside.

Logan's shoes pounded the floor as he ran with Rogue and her friends through a downstairs hallway and rounded a corner. In front of them, Pyro slammed to a halt and opened a secret passage. The kids scrambled inside. But Logan waited, listening to the approaching soldiers.

"Keep going," Logan told them, motioning for them to move.

Rogue didn't budge. "Logan," she pleaded, biting her lip.

He stared at her, an animalistic gleam in his eye. *Don't argue with me,* it said. He knew she would listen. She blinked back tears as the passage door shut.

He turned around. *Snikt!* His claws popped out.

Suddenly, through the smoke, a dozen green lasers trained on Logan's body. Soldiers surrounded him in a semicircle.

Anger and passion and loathing raged through him. "You wanna shoot me?" he bellowed. "Shoot me!" He barreled forward, about to cut into them, when—

"Don't shoot him," came a calm male voice. A man stepped into the hallway, emerging through the smoke. The soldiers parted to let him pass.

Logan froze.

"Not yet," the voice added as Logan tried to peer through the darkness at the approaching figure.

"Wolverine," the man said. "How long has it been? Fifteen years? And you haven't changed a bit. Me, on the other hand . . ."

A man stepped into the light. "Nature."

Logan searched the man's aged face, triggering a vague memory.

Involuntarily, his claws slowly retracted.

Professor X

Cyclops

Rogue

Wolverine experiences Cerebro with the professor.

Stryker is prepared for a global battle.

Nightcrawler!

Stryker's soldiers are no match for Wolverine.

Bobby and Rogue watch as their school is invaded.

Professor X pays a visit to Magneto's plastic prison.

The school is under siege!

Bobby uses his powers for good.

The X-Jet is in Dr Grey's and Storm's hands.

Cyclops lashes out at Magneto's cell.

"Wait," Rogue said, stopping at the head of the passageway. "You've got to do something." She fought back tears. "They're going to kill him."

She watched in dismay as Pyro backed away. "He can handle himself. Let's go."

"Bobby, please!" she begged desperately. Her boyfriend looked at Pyro, then back at her, torn.

For Rogue there was no question. Logan had saved her life. She wouldn't let someone take his.

—X2—

"I must admit, this is the last place I thought I'd ever see you, Wolverine," the man said, moving closer. Logan could feel his breath, warm on his skin. "I didn't realize Xavier was taking in animals." The man studied him. "Even animals as unique as you."

Logan gave him a hard look. "Who are you?"

The man smirked at him. "Don't you remember?"

Logan stared at him, searching for some familiar sign, something he could recognize.

Suddenly the space between the two of them began to fade. A thin wall of white fog was starting to form in the room. Soon Logan couldn't see the man at all. He was completely obscured by mist . . . mist that became a thick wall of ice.

Logan startled as he turned to see Rogue and Bobby emerge from the passageway. Bobby's frost-covered hand was on the wall.

"Logan, come on," Rogue urged, her face white.

"Go," he said. "I'll be fine."

"But we won't," Rogue shot back. "Please."

Seconds later the man on the other side of the ice wall grabbed a grenade and jammed it into the ice. The wall exploded. But when the ice collapsed and the mist cleared, Logan and his friends were gone.

—X2—

Minutes later Logan and the teenagers were running through one of the X-Mansion's escape tunnels. Following Bobby's lead, they turned down one tunnel and found themselves in a large garage. Automatic lights clicked on, illuminating a dozen or so extremely expensive sports cars.

Everyone scrambled into the sports coupe closest to the garage door. Logan scowled as Pyro slid behind the driver's seat. "I'm driving," Pyro said.

In your dreams. Logan yanked him out. "In the back, buddy."

Grumbling, Pyro got in the back with Bobby while Rogue slid in beside Logan.

"This is Cyclops's car," Bobby announced.

"Oh yeah?" Logan said. *Snikt!* A claw shot out from his hand, piercing the ignition. The car roared to life. Logan stepped on the gas.

They were off. Logan let the car fly down the road, his mind racing almost as fast as the engine. Who was invading the X-Mansion, and why? He felt as if the answer were right in front of him, dancing in front of his grasp.

"You could slow down you know," Bobby huffed as the car hugged a tight curve. Logan went even faster. Chances were slim to none that he'd ever drive a car like this again. He wanted to take full advantage.

"What the hell was that back there?" Pyro asked, looking back over his shoulder.

"Stryker," Logan said slowly. "His name is Stryker."

Rogue's eyes were filled with worry. "Who is he?"

Logan struggled to piece it together. "I don't remember." He stared out at the twisting road in front of him, trees and houses rushing past. Then he glanced over at Rogue. She was playing with something on her wrist. It was his dog tag, engraved WOLVERINE.

Rogue looked up. She blinked. Logan turned back to the road. Then he felt a small metal object push against his wrist.

Rogue had pulled the dog tag off and was handing it to him. He hesitated for a second, then reached out and grabbed the tag, rubbing his finger over the imprinted metal.

Suddenly loud techno music pulsated through the cramped space.

"What are you doing?" Rogue snapped, watching as Pyro fiddled with the radio knob.

"I don't like uncomfortable silence," he retorted.

Logan gripped the steering wheel, trying to stay cool as the music grew louder and louder. Finally Pyro pressed the CD player's Eject button, and a tray slid open, revealing a small oval-shaped disc. Pyro grabbed it, but the music kept coming. To Logan's relief, Rogue hit a series of buttons, one of which stopped the music.

Pyro examined the disc, then pressed another button on the dashboard. A door clicked open, revealing a compartment containing a hi-tech-looking communication device.

"I don't think this is the CD player," he said.

Logan yanked the disc from Pyro. There weren't any markings on it. Not sure what it was, he stuffed it in his pocket.

"So where are we going?" Pyro piped up.

"Storm and Jean are in Boston. We'll head that way," Logan told them.

"My parents live in Boston," Bobby offered.

"Good," Logan said curtly as the car flew down the highway. They were going to need all the help they could get.

X2

Stryker and his operational assault force leader, Lyman, walked quickly down the deserted X-Mansion corridor, dressed in combat gear.

"Sir, most of the mutants escaped through tunnels that weren't in the schematics, but we have several in custody," Lyman said, trying to match Stryker's rapid pace.

"How many?"

"Six, sir," Lyman told him.

"Pack them up," Stryker ordered as they rounded the corner. A door stood ajar. It was the door to Cerebro. Capturing the mutants was all well and good . . . but this was the real prize.

Stryker watched as two soldiers worked to set up a small device on a tripod in front of the blue crystal lock, at the exact height Professor X's eyes would be. The soldiers turned on the device, and Cerebro hummed to life.

A blue laser shot out from the lock and hit a small crystal on the front of the device. Stryker held his breath.

The blue laser split into a set of smaller beams. The crystal rotated back and forth, changing the shape of the laser, trying to find the proper configuration. Finally, the device beeped. The blue laser shut off, and the heavy metal vault door to Cerebro slid open.

"Welcome, Professor."

It was Cerebro.

Stryker grinned as he walked down the platform to the center of the chamber, surveying the scene.

Cerebro was his.

—X2—

The bar TV was blaring some nonsense about mutant rights as Mitchell Laurio sat down at an empty table in his local watering hole. He loosened his shirt and tie and emptied the dregs from his beer glass. He'd had a rough day, and watching two morons spout off about the Mutant Registration Act was more than he could stomach. "Turn that crap off, Lou," he told the bartender, who silently obliged.

"Got a lot on your mind, huh?"

Laurio turned. Standing at the bar was the most beautiful woman he had ever seen. Shiny black hair, gorgeous blue eyes, and legs that were long and lean.

Maybe his day was about to turn around.

She peered carefully at his name tag. "Mr. Laurio?" Her voice was soft and breathy.

Laurio smiled, his eyes widening as he took her in.

"I'm Grace," she said, purring slightly. "Want another beer?" She sat down across from him and slid a fresh frothy mug over. "Of course you do."

They hit it off immediately. Laurio's weary eyes never left her. Not that they would have detected the two small white pills at the bottom of the beer mug anyway.

Soon "Grace" had cajoled him into following her into the dingy barroom bathroom, where, in a matter of minutes, Laurio was passed out . . . and Grace was no longer Grace. She was Mystique. And she had accomplished the mission Magneto had sent her to perform. A syringeful of metallic liquid was now swimming its way through Mitchell Laurio's bloodstream.

CHAPTER EIGHT

STRYKER'S BASE

Back at Stryker's base, Professor X sat in his wheelchair, his wrists tied to the armrests. Some sort of electrical band had been wrapped around his head. They had placed him in a dark, cramped room—a cell, really. The only way out was the door in front of him.

If only he could focus, perhaps— *BUZZZTTT!* A sharp pain shot into his skull, jolting him upright. Unable to lift his arm to massage the pain, the professor blinked back tears, then opened his eyes to see Stryker standing in front of him, chuckling.

"I call it the Neural Inhibitor," he explained, indicating the headband.

Stryker strolled into the cell, Yuriko Oyama at his heels. He touched his head. "It keeps *you* out of *here.*"

Professor X steadied himself. "William."

"Please, Xavier." Stryker smirked. "Don't get up." He pulled up a chair and sat down in front of him.

"What have you done with Scott?" the professor asked, trying to fight the urge to think but not knowing what else he could do.

"Don't worry. I'm just giving him a little re-education," he said. His eyes narrowed. "But you know all about that, don't you?"

Professor X shook his head slightly. It was taking every last bit of his energy just to form a coherent thought. "You wanted me to cure your son, William," he said weakly. "But mutation isn't a disease. It's—"

"You're lying, Xavier," Stryker spat. "You were more frightened of him than I was!"

The professor took a deep breath as Yuriko cracked her knuckles. He looked over at her. There was something about her. . . .

Stryker stood up. "You know, just one year after Jason returned from your school, my wife, unhinged by constant contact with him, took a power drill to her left temple." He leaned in. "She was attempting to bore out the images he was projecting into her mind."

Yuriko's breathing had become erratic. She was shaking her head slightly now, as if waking up from a dream. She looked around the room, confused.

Xavier tilted his head toward the young woman. "For

someone who hates mutants, you certainly keep strange company."

Stryker looked at Yuriko. A smile crept across his thin lips. "They serve their purpose. For now."

Professor X watched in horror as Stryker removed a vial of yellow liquid from his pocket and placed two large drops on a circular scar on the nape of her neck. As the liquid seeped in, the woman's breathing steadied and she grew calm once more. Stryker whispered something in her ear. She nodded and quickly left the room.

Slowly it began to dawn on him. "You arranged the attack on the president."

"And you didn't even have to read my mind," Stryker said in a singsong voice. "You know, I've been working with mutants as long as you have, Xavier, and the most frustrating thing I've learned is that nobody really knows how many even exist . . . or how to find them." He stopped. "Except you." He held up the vial.

"Unfortunately this little potion won't work on *you*, will it?" Stryker said, backing up and returning the vial to his pocket. "No, no, you're much too *powerful* for that. Instead, we'll go right to the source."

Professor X watched as Stryker opened the door behind him. A shriveled, emaciated man sat in a wheelchair. Syringes and tubes ran from his head into clear containers on the back of his chair, collecting a yellow fluid from his spinal column.

Xavier felt dizzy. The yellow fluid in the vial wasn't a

drug . . . it was a chemical extracted from the grotesque shell of a person who now sat in front of him.

Stryker smiled. "Allow me to introduce Mutant 143."

The professor looked at the wretched mutant's face. He had one bright blue eye and one bright green eye, and a giant scar ran across his forehead. Could it be? "Jason?" he forced out. Then he turned his appalled eyes to Stryker. "My God, William. This is your *son*. What have you done to him?"

Stryker was cold as he looked at Mutant 143, sadly shaking his head. "No, *Charles*," he corrected him. "My son is dead." He turned to walk away. "Just like the rest of you."

Professor X closed his eyes as the door slammed shut. Pain throttled his head, making him gasp. But the only person who heard him was William Stryker's forsaken son, Mutant 143. Jason Stryker.

CHAPTER NINE

BOSTON, MASSACHUSETTS

Rogue had secretly hoped she might be able to meet Bobby's family one day, but she'd imagined that she'd be wearing clothes—not a see-through nightie. She shifted uncomfortably from one foot to the other as Bobby grabbed a key from the top of the doorjamb and unlocked his family's house. She and Logan and Pyro followed him into the dark foyer.

"Mom? Dad?" Bobby called tentatively, peering around. "Ronnie? Anybody home?"

The house was silent. "I'll try to find you some clothes," he told Rogue. "Don't burn anything," he warned Pyro, who scowled.

Logan decided to wait in the kitchen while Pyro swaggered into the living room. Rogue followed Bobby upstairs and hung out in his room while he went in search of an outfit.

Snowboarding posters lined the walls, and a good-sized collection of CDs was stacked next to a stereo. It was strange to think of Bobby living in this room, eating dinner in this house. . . . It brought back memories of the nonmutant world she too had fled. With a sad shake of her head, she tied her long hair back into a ponytail and began thumbing through the CDs.

Bobby was back in a flash. "Hey. I think they were my mom's, from before I was born." He handed her a white peasant top with embroidery around the neckline and a pair of jeans.

Rogue's eyes twinkled. "Groovy." She turned her back and quickly changed.

"And these were my grandmother's," Bobby said, clearing his throat. Rogue looked over. He held a beautiful pair of long opera gloves.

As Rogue reached for them, Bobby tried to touch her finger gently. Instinctively she pulled back, flinching.

"You know I would never hurt you," Bobby whispered, his brown eyes tender.

"I know," Rogue whispered back.

"And you won't hurt me," he promised.

Rogue looked into his eyes. She was excited and frightened and, well, eager. Before she could think it through anymore, she was closing her eyes and leaning forward and kissing him. His lips were soft and gentle and perfect. *So this is what it feels like,* she thought dreamily. They pulled back, staring at each other.

Rogue let out a cold, frosty breath of air. And then they kissed again. This time it was deeper. Longer. It felt just as wonderful. *Why have we waited so long?* Rogue wondered. Bobby was right. She wasn't—

"Unhhh." Bobby ripped his lips away from her mouth and sat down hard on the bed. His face was drained of color and contorted with pain.

Rogue blinked back tears. "I'm sorry," she squeaked, mortified.

Bobby wouldn't meet her watery eyes. "It's okay," he mumbled.

—X2—

How the heck does this thing work? I need to reach Jean. Logan pushed button after button on the two-way communication device he'd found in Cyclops's car, but nothing he did garnered any kind of response. He'd managed to get part of it to open, but that had gotten him nowhere.

Agitated, he opened the fridge and pulled out a beer. *At last, I get a beer tonight,* he thought as he shut the door.

Wham! A flurry of black fur was in front of him. *Snikt!* Logan's claws shot out. Then he laughed. It was a silly old cat. The cat nudged itself against Logan, licking his claws.

He was so taken with the cat's antics that he didn't hear a car pull up or the sound of footsteps outside. When the front door opened, he was caught completely off guard.

An older, well-dressed couple, presumably the Drakes, and a boy slightly younger than Bobby stood gaping at him. Logan was barely able to retract his claws in time.

"Who are you?" Mr. Drake shouted.

Logan stood rooted to the spot, clutching his beer, as Bobby and Rogue came tearing down the stairs.

"Honey, aren't you supposed to be at school?" a bewildered Mrs. Drake asked Bobby.

Mr. Drake's eyebrows bunched together. "Bobby, who is this guy?"

Bobby licked his lips. "Mom, Dad . . . this is Professor Logan."

Mrs. Drake gave Rogue an irritated once-over. "What is she doing wearing my clothes?"

Professor Logan watched as Bobby shuffled his feet together. "Uh, can I talk to you about something?"

—**X2**—

That babe Grace sure had made Mitchell Laurio's night last night. She was what he called a real woman. Nothing could put him in a bad mood today. Not even having to sit around in this plastic prison and watch that weird Magneto read that dumb book.

"What's that on your face, Mitch?" asked one of the guards as he walked past the security checkpoint.

Laurio gave him a toothy grin as he balanced Magneto's food tray. "Satisfaction."

He was waved through clearance. Soon he stood in front of the napping Master of Magnetism. "Have a nice sleep, Lensherr?" he drawled as he put the food on a plastic table.

Magneto scrutinized him. "There's something different about you, Mr. Laurio." He sat up, trying to get a closer look.

Laurio smirked. "Yeah, I was actually having a good day."

Magneto stood up, staring at Laurio. It gave him the creeps.

"No, no . . . ," Magneto surmised. "It's not that."

"Sit down," Laurio ordered, not liking the way Magneto was suddenly so interested in him.

"No," Magneto said.

Laurio pulled out his billy club. "Sit your butt down or I'll—"

Magneto held up his arm. A chill ran through Laurio's body. His hand opened and dropped the club. "What could it be?" Magneto murmured.

All of a sudden Laurio was lifted off his feet. He hovered a foot above the ground, his legs arching behind him. He let out a terrified scream. *What the hell is going on?*

"Ah, there it is," Magneto said, satisfied. He slashed his hand in a sharp zigzag motion, and a mist of blood burst from Laurio's body. "Too much iron in your blood."

Laurio felt weak, drained. He watched, terrified, as the misty red cloud fell away, leaving a cluster of metal particles hovering in the air.

Magneto squeezed his hand into a fist, and the metal compressed into three balls, each the size of a marble. Drops of blood—*My blood,* Laurio thought dizzily—oozed from each. The balls began to move, orbiting Magneto's palm.

"Mr. Laurio, never trust a beautiful woman. Especially one that is interested in you."

The woman—Grace—it had all been some sort of trick. A plot hatched by this evil magnetic mutant. Laurio's eyes rolled. He couldn't fight it any longer. The marble balls smashed through the plastic wall. Alarms rang. And Mitchell Laurio slumped to the ground.

If he'd been awake, he would have seen the balls whiz through the cell, shattering walls and security cameras. He would have watched as the guards tried desperately to contain Magneto. In a panic, they'd retracted the catwalk from Magneto's cell. But they were boys playing a man's game. Magneto let one of the balls glide to his feet and flatten to become a large, thin silver disk. He stepped on it and it floated across the abyss, toward the plastic door on the other side.

The guards ran for their lives.

And Magneto's metal balls—composed of the metal Mystique had injected into Mitchell Laurio's bloodstream—shot forward and shattered the door that had kept him in a plastic prison cell for far too long.

—X2—

Storm tried to fight back the worry that threatened to overcome her. Jean had been trying to contact the X-Mansion for a half hour, and all she was getting was static on the X-Jet radio.

A faint whisper made her look back over her shoulder. Nightcrawler's eyes were closed tight and his hands were folded. He was deep in prayer.

Leaving Jean at the controls, Storm walked toward him, staring at the tattoos on his face. She'd never seen anything like them.

Sensing her presence and seemingly able to read her mind, Nightcrawler said, "They're angelic symbols." His yellow eyes opened and lit on her. "Passed on to mankind by the archangel Gabriel."

"They're beautiful," Storm told him sincerely. "How many do you have?"

"One for every sin," Nightcrawler said. "So, quite a few." He gazed around the X-Jet, then back at Storm in her black leather uniform. "You and Ms. Grey, you're both . . . schoolteachers?"

"Yes, at a school for people like us," Storm told him. "Where we can be . . . safe."

Nightcrawler seemed perplexed. "From what?"

"Everyone else," Storm said. Wasn't that obvious?

"You know, outside of the circus, most people were afraid of me, but I never hated them," Nightcrawler admitted. "I pitied them. Do you know why?"

Storm shook her head. The injustices that mutants had to suffer gave her great pain.

"Because most people never know anything beyond what they can see with their own two eyes."

It was a nice sentiment, but Storm couldn't accept it. "I gave up on pity a long time ago," she said bitterly.

She didn't move as Nightcrawler reached out to caress her cheek. "Someone as beautiful as you shouldn't be so angry."

"Anger can help you survive."

"So can faith," he persisted.

"Storm?" It was Jean, from the cockpit. Storm turned. "I found an active com device."

Bobby shot his parents a nervous glance. They were sitting on the couch across from him and Rogue. They didn't look very happy. His brother, Ronnie, wouldn't even look at him. He didn't expect a coming-out party, though. They were a pretty conventional family.

"So . . . ," his mom said, her finger tracing the rim of her teacup. "When did you first know . . . that you were a . . . um . . ."

"A mutant?" Pyro filled in. He leaned on an end table and flicked his lighter.

Bobby's mother frowned over at his lighter. "Could you please stop that?"

His father rubbed his temples. "You have to understand, we thought Bobby was going to a school for the gifted."

He could feel Rogue shift beside him. "Bobby is gifted," she told them, giving his arm a reassuring squeeze.

But his father brushed her words aside. "We know that. We just didn't realize that he was—"

"We still love you, Bobby," his mother cut in. "It's just that the mutant problem is very—"

Logan put down the beer he was nursing. "What mutant problem?" he said, his brows drawing together.

"Complicated," his mother finished, looking to her husband for guidance.

Bobby's father gave Logan a dark look. "Excuse me, what exactly are you a professor of, Mr. Logan?"

"Art." Logan took a drink. "And it's just Logan."

Cringing inside, Bobby tried to think of a way to get out of there. Why had he ever thought going home was a good idea?

"You should see what Bobby can do," Rogue offered, her eyes filled with hope.

He swallowed, looking at his parents. Then he reached across the table and touched his mother's cup. Instantly it was covered with a thin layer of frost.

"Bobby!" His mother gasped as he turned the teacup over and a frozen dome of tea plopped onto the saucer. He smiled as his cat jumped on the table and gave the icy blob a lick.

His father was actually smiling. "I can do a lot more than that," Bobby told them, buoyed. Maybe there was a glimmer of hope.

He started as his brother got up and stormed upstairs.

"Ronnie!" his mother called fretfully after him.

The only answer they heard was the sound of a door slamming.

His mother wouldn't let it go. "Oh, this is all my fault," she moaned, cradling her head in her hands.

"Actually, they've discovered that males are the ones who

carry mutant genes and pass them on to the next generation," Pyro told her, a hint of glee in his eyes. "So actually it's his fault," he said, pointing to Bobby's father.

Bobby winced at his dad's mortified expression.

"And you," his mother said, looking at his friends. "You're all gifted?"

Everyone nodded as his mother tried to put on a happy face. A few more awkward moments went by.

Suddenly Bobby heard a beeping noise coming from Logan's pocket.

"That's for me," the Wolverine said, taking the cell phone out and walking to the backyard.

Bobby's mother moved closer. "Have you tried not being a mutant?" she asked earnestly.

He sighed. There was no hope.

—X2—

"Professor?" Logan said, speaking into the cell phone.

"Logan, thank God." It was Jean. "We couldn't reach anyone at the mansion."

Logan paced back and forth. "No one's left, Jean. Soldiers came."

"And the children?" This time it was Storm. They must have put him on speakerphone.

A vision of Colossus carrying students into the tunnel

flashed into his mind. "Some of them escaped, but I'm not sure about the rest."

Jean's voice crackled through the phone. "We haven't been able to reach the professor or Scott either."

"Where are you?" Storm asked.

Logan glanced around at the backyard, with its barbecue and neatly tended geraniums. "Boston, with Bobby Drake's family."

"All right, we're on our way," Storm told him.

Logan could see the Drakes through the living room window. He wasn't sure how much more the Drakes—or Bobby—could take. "And Storm? Make it fast." He clicked the phone off and stepped toward the sliding glass door. But as he started to go inside, he stopped. He smelled something. Something living. He closed the door again. He could see the reflection of people creeping up behind him in the glass.

He slammed the door open, then bolted inside and locked the door behind him. "We have to go now," he said to the kids.

"Why?" Rogue asked, confused.

"Now." Snikt! His claws popped out.

Rogue was scared now. "Logan, what's going on?"

There was no time. They headed toward the front door, then burst onto the front porch.

Click! Two policemen were there, waiting. They cocked

their guns at Logan and the kids. More police were emerging from their cars, which were parked haphazardly on the front lawn.

"Ronnie," Bobby muttered under his breath.

Logan glanced back at the house. Sure enough, there was Bobby's brother, staring out the window with a small smile on his face.

"Get down on the ground!" barked one of the cops. The rest of the cops began moving toward them.

Logan didn't move. "What's going on here?"

Bobby and Rogue looked terrified as a cop headed their way.

"Put down the knives," the cop told Logan. "Slowly."

That wasn't going to be possible. "Hey, bub, this is just a misunderstanding," Logan insisted, backing up.

More cops had gone up to the house. "Open the door!" they yelled to the Drakes, who stood bewildered and terrified inside. Logan groaned inwardly as one of the cops smashed open the door with his nightstick and stormed inside.

"Put the knives down!" the cop in front of Logan repeated, his face reddening.

"I can't!" Logan shouted. Couldn't the guy see that they were part of him? Maybe he couldn't. To illustrate his predicament, Logan raised his arms to show the cop that the claws were attached to his hands.

Bang! Something small and hot and hard hit him in the

head. A wet trickle slid down his cheek. With Rogue's anguished screams ringing in his ears, he fell over.

—X2—

Pyro had had enough of this. What had he done to any of these people? What had Logan done to deserve getting shot in the head? He looked at the cop, whose gun was still smoking. This was a bunch of crap.

He watched as Rogue and Bobby followed the cop's orders and slowly started to kneel, hands behind their heads.

No way was he going to do that. No way.

He stood there, flicking his lighter faster and faster.

One of the cops walked over to him. "We don't wanna hurt you, kid," he said.

Pyro flicked his lighter again. "You know all those dangerous mutants you hear about on the news?" he called out to the cops. "I'm the worst one." He lowered his head. *Flick*. The small flame on his lighter shot out in massive streams. One shot to the left. One shot to the right. And one raced behind him into the Drakes' house.

Floosh! The cops in the living room were knocked down with a blast of burning flame.

Power surged through Pyro's veins. This was what it was all

about. They wanted to hurt innocent mutants? It was payback time.

His eyes narrowed as streams of flames shot out toward two police cruisers. *Boom!* The cars exploded, tumbling and spinning in the air. Cops were squawking on their walkie-talkies, diving for cover. Only one police car remained. Flames swirled and danced around it as the two officers inside tried to radio for backup. Pyro cackled, watching as pieces of the car melted before their eyes.

Sweat poured down Pyro's face. Melting tires . . . *I did this.* . . . Crackling glass . . . *No one can hurt me.* . . . Flames surrounding the car . . . *Don't mess with me.* . . .

Unleashing his power like this, using his ability . . . the feeling was indescribable. He held up the lighter once more—

"Ahhh!" he cried, light flashing on his skin. Rogue had snuck up on him, pulling up on his pants and grabbing his bare leg. His heart palpitated in his chest. The incredible power rush reversed, and Pyro felt all his energy being sucked away.

Gasping, he dropped his lighter and slumped to the ground. He watched, breathing hard, as Rogue held up her hand and concentrated. The flames Pyro had caused immediately died, leaving smoldering debris.

Rogue let out a relieved sigh as she helped pull Bobby to his feet.

Pyro groaned. He grabbed his lighter and got up. He

surveyed the scene that he had caused. Sure, he was weak and dazed and tired. But with the sweet aftertaste of power lingering on his lips, all was not lost.

—X2—

The bullet, flattened against Logan's metal skull, dislodged and fell to the ground. His body began to heal itself, and by the time Pyro's firefest was over, Logan was completely whole again.

He was on his feet when thunder crackled in the sky above them and the lawn was blasted by a heavy wind. Seconds later, amidst pelting rain, the X-Jet landed in the street. He and the kids ran to it.

One of the cops pulled out his gun and aimed directly at Logan. Logan stared him down. And kept on moving.

He felt a momentary pang for Bobby as the Drakes looked on in shock. But there wasn't time for pity or sadness. There was only time for action.

Logan bounded onto the jet and strapped himself into a plush leather seat. Jean smiled at him from the copilot's chair.

He gave her a wink.

And then his jaw dropped when a scaly blue-faced man popped up from behind one of the chairs.

"Guten Morgen," the mutant said. He gave Logan a jaunty nod.

"*Guten* Abend," Logan snarled back. "Who the hell are you?"

He made a dramatic wave with his hand. "Kurt Wagner, but in the Munich circus I was known as 'The Incredible Nightcraw—'"

"Save it." Logan cut him off curtly. "Storm?"

Storm's eyes flashed. Thunder rolled. "We're out of here." She pulled hard on the control stick.

And the X-Jet lifted off.

CHAPTER TEN

THE X-MANSION?

Professor X looked out the open bay window. In front of him lay the X-Mansion's large, expansive gardens. The sun shone brightly. Birds fluttered in the trees. A honeybee landed on the petal of a large red rose.

In front of him sat a chess set, its pieces apparently mid-game. Xavier looked down at his legs. There was no wheelchair.

He was standing.

Professor X concentrated hard, rubbing his head. *This isn't right; this can't be. . . .*

He closed his eyes and gritted his teeth. *I am in a wheelchair. I cannot stand.* It was all an illusion created by Stryker's mutant son. "Jason, stop it!"

The room began to ripple, the plush surroundings of the

X-Mansion twisting and fading into what was really true: the bleakness of his cell, deep inside Stryker's base. He wasn't standing. He was sitting in his wheelchair, directly across from Mutant 143.

Xavier opened his eyes, remembering where he was. The neural inhibitor that was clamped onto his head began to buzz wildly. He gripped the armrests, trying to bear the pain.

"You must help me," he gritted out.

"You must help me," Mutant 143 mimicked. Then the young mutant moved toward the professor, reaching for his throat.

Xavier didn't flinch. He stared deep into the other mutant's blue and green eyes, gripping his chair, fighting the pain that engulfed him.

"Stand," the professor murmured.

"Stand," Mutant 143 repeated thickly. He stood up, and the spinal connector popped out of place. Yellow liquid leaked from the tiny wound at the back of his neck. Mutant 143 reached forward and gently removed the neural inhibitor from the professor's head.

The pain dissolved. Xavier let out a sigh of release. "Thank you, Jason," he murmured gratefully.

"Thank you, Jason," Mutant 143 echoed faintly.

The professor reached up and touched 143's cheek. Pity washed over him for this young mutant, so brutally treated by his own father. Jason dropped back into his seat, his face glazing over into a blank slate.

Filled with determination, the professor wheeled himself to the door, concentrating hard. "Mr. Smith, are you there?"

The door opened, revealing two young soldiers. They turned to face him, their minds falling under his control.

"I arrived here with a friend," Xavier said firmly as one of the soldiers removed his arm restraints. "Take me to him."

Moments later they were at Cyclops's cell. The soldiers brought Cyclops his visor.

"What is the quickest way out of here?" the professor asked them as Cyclops steadied his visor.

"The helicopter," said one of the soldiers in a monotone.

Xavier's mouth was grim. "Take us there, now."

—X2—

"How far are we?" Logan asked, stepping into the X-Jet's cockpit.

"We're coming up on the mansion now," Jean replied.

A flight-deck monitor began beeping. Two small red blips flashed.

"I've got two signals approaching," Storm announced, steadying her hands. The signals were two F-16 fighter jets. They roared through the clouds, coming up behind the X-Jet.

Jean peered out the window. The fighters flanked them now. The radio crackled.

"Unidentified aircraft, you are ordered to descend to twenty thousand feet and return with our escort to Hanscom Air Force Base," came the voice of an F-16 pilot over the radio. "Failure to comply will result in the use of extreme force."

Storm clicked her teeth. "Somebody's angry."

Logan glared at Pyro, who sat impassively in the rear of the aircraft. "I wonder why."

Beep! Beep, beep!

"They're marking us," Storm cried out, frightened. "They're going to fire. Seat belts!"

The X-Jet banked and dove, trying to shake off the fighters.

Reesht! Missiles shot off from each F-16. The X-Jet banked hard and rolled to the side, narrowly dodging the exploding missiles.

But the fighter jets were still on their tail.

Nightcrawler quickly made the sign of the cross as Bobby and Rogue tried not to panic.

"Don't we have any weapons in this heap?" Logan shouted.

Storm's eyes burned white. Dark, rumbling clouds began to form in front of the X-Jet. Lightning flashed. The jet headed straight into the eye of the growing storm caused by Storm's wrath. The F-16s were right behind it.

Soon wispy clouds began to swirl, faster and faster, twisting into long, thin funnels. Storm's intensity grew. One funnel formed. Then another. The sky was filled with dozens of roaring tornadoes, writhing like giant serpents.

The women deftly navigated the X-Jet through the tornadoes. But the F-16s weren't as lucky. They darted and weaved, trying to avoid getting sucked into a whirling funnel.

Boom! Two tornadoes slammed into one of the F-16s, yanking it up and hurling it across the sky. The massive fighter plane tumbled like a toy. Storm looked out the window and saw the pilot eject. The other plane managed to swerve around the funnel cloud.

The radar screen beeped over and over. Storm could feel her anger bubbling up inside.

The clouds around the remaining F-16 began to swirl. Within seconds the plane was completely encased in a long, dark funnel cloud, a tornado that stretched across the sky. It began to roll wildly, banking from left to right and losing control. Somehow, the pilot managed to fire two more missiles. Then he ejected, the F-16 spiraled to the ground . . . and the missiles whizzed through the storm and continued on their path.

Storm yanked the control stick back, her hands cold and clammy. Two blips were rushing toward them on the radar screen. Her eyes burned even whiter. Her anger could create a powerful storm . . . but it wasn't within her power to halt missiles.

The X-Jet's wings folded up as it flew faster, leaving the storm in its wake. The missiles continued their trajectory. But then, suddenly, one of them began to wobble. *Jean!* Storm realized suddenly. Dr. Grey could use her power to make the missiles change course. *She can save us!*

Storm looked intently at the radar screen. *The blips are getting closer!* She whipped her gaze to Jean and saw her friend staring at the radar screen, lost in a trance.

"Jean?" she said fearfully as Dr. Grey held her head tightly.

Outside the X-Jet, the missile wobbled. A few lights on its surface blinked off. Then, without warning, it veered straight up and exploded.

One down, one to go, Storm thought, trying to stay calm. She watched as Jean closed her eyes. She knew she was using all her powers to stop the remaining missile. There was nothing to do but wait.

Storm's eyes darted toward the radar screen. The second missile was getting closer.

"Oh, God," Jean murmured.

Then Storm could no longer hear her own thoughts in her mind, and the world fell apart as the missile slammed into the X-Jet.

Clouds of fire and smoke billowed in the cockpit. Storm heard someone screaming, then realized it was her own terrified self. Gushes of cold night air streamed into the jet. *But how . . . ?* Storm looked up. To her horror, a large hole gaped in the roof of the X-Jet. Suddenly the plane began to decompress. Shrieking wind drowned out the screams of the X-Men.

Then, before her very eyes, Storm watched as Rogue was ripped from her seat and sucked out of the hole.

There wasn't time to move or cry or reach for her. She was gone!

And then Nightcrawler disappeared, and moments later, *bamf!* he was back—with a wide-eyed Rogue in his blue-skinned arms.

Wind whipping her hair against her face, Storm fought alongside Jean to regain control of the X-Jet. If they could stabilize the plane, they still had a chance.

Three thousand feet. Two thousand five hundred feet. The altimeter told the truth—and the truth was they were plummeting to Earth with dizzying speed.

Storm strained against the controls, trying to pull out of the nosedive. But it was useless. She closed her eyes, bracing herself. *This is it.*

"Uh, Storm?" came Nightcrawler's voice.

She turned. The mutant pointed at the torn roof. The hole was bending and twisting, slowly repairing itself. The screaming wind faded to nothingness as the hole closed completely. The falling plane began to reduce its speed.

"Jean?" Storm cried, stunned.

"It's not me," Jean said slowly.

The ground got closer. Closer. And then, in nosedive position, fifteen feet off the ground, the X-Jet stopped.

Storm looked at the faces of her fellow mutants. They were just as confused and shocked as she was.

She peered out the windshield. She could make out a forest clearing—and two figures staring up at them.

Magneto stood in front of the X-Jet, holding it in place with an outstretched hand. Mystique stood alongside him.

The Master of Magnetism locked eyes with Storm. Then he spoke. "If I set you down gently, will you hear me out?"

CHAPTER ELEVEN

THE WOODS— later that night

The campfire light flickered on the faces of the X-Men. Jean wrapped her arms around her body and stared across the burning embers at Magneto and Mystique.

"His name is William Stryker," Magneto began.

Jean could feel Logan stiffen beside her.

"What does he want?" she asked.

Storm's face was stony. "That's the same question we should be asking Magneto." She studied him. "So what is it? What do *you* want?"

Magneto sighed. "When Stryker invaded your mansion, he stole an essential piece of its hardware."

Jean let out a gasp. "Cerebro." The implications were

terrifying. "But Stryker would need the professor to operate it," she said feebly, glancing nervously at Storm.

"Which is the only reason I think he's still alive," Magneto told them.

Cold, hard fear balled up in Jean's stomach. If Cerebro was in the hands of someone like Stryker, then—

"What are you all so afraid of?" Logan asked suddenly, searching her face for an explanation.

Magneto spoke up. "While Cerebro is working, Charles's mind is connected to every living person on the planet. If he were to concentrate on a particular group . . ." He hesitated. "Let's say mutants, for example . . . he could kill us all."

"How would Stryker know what Cerebro is, or where to find it?" Storm wondered aloud.

Magneto paused. Then, slowly, he lifted his arm and rubbed the back of his neck. Jean saw a small, circular scar there.

His eyes dropped. "Because I told him. I helped Charles build it, remember?" For a moment Magneto actually looked ashamed. "Mr. Stryker has powerful methods of persuasion. Even against a mutant as strong as Charles."

"Who is Stryker, anyway?" Jean asked him. Magneto might be many things, but Jean was certain he was being honest with them.

"A military scientist who has spent his life looking for a solution to the mutant problem," Magneto replied. "But if you want a more intimate perspective, why don't you ask the Wolverine?"

The X-Men all turned to Logan.

"You don't remember," Magneto said, more of a statement than a question.

Jean flinched at the glare Logan gave Magneto.

"William Stryker is the only other man I know who can manipulate adamantium," Magneto told them, his face shining with orange firelight. "The metal on your bones? It carries *his* signature."

"But the professor—" Logan began.

"The professor trusted you were smart enough to discover this on your own. He gives you more credit than I do," Magneto said imperiously.

Jean sat there, trying to take it all in. Stryker was responsible for turning Logan into the Wolverine.

"Why do you need us?" Storm spoke out.

"Mystique discovered plans for a base that Stryker's been operating out of for decades," he said. "But we don't know where it is. And I believe one of you might."

"The professor already tried," Logan told him.

Magneto sighed. "Once again, you think it's all about you."

Jean closed her eyes. What was it all about? The destruction of mutants everywhere? Magneto had voiced her ultimate fear. So what was she going to be able to do to prevent it from becoming reality?

Rogue dusted off her hands and stood back, surveying her work. The stove was small, but at least they could cook spaghetti or something on it. That was, if they could ever get a fire going.

Nightcrawler pushed a few buttons, then shook his head as Bobby attempted to get it started.

"You *could* help, you know," Rogue told Pyro, barely keeping the annoyance from her voice. All he had done was lounge about, watching them struggle and never lifting a finger.

Whoosh! Rogue blinked as the stove erupted into a gigantic flame. Bobby jumped back. Rogue shook her head. At times she felt like Pyro was on their side—but he did such stupid stuff that she wasn't quite sure.

As the guys continued to shoot one another dirty looks, Rogue glanced over at the X-Men and the campfire. They had been sitting there for a long time. She was dying to know what they were talking about.

"Can you hear what they're saying?" Nightcrawler asked, moving beside her.

Frustrated, she shook her head.

"I can get a closer look," Nightcrawler offered, looking a bit embarrassed.

"How?"

Bamf! Nightcrawler disappeared in a cloud of smoke. Seconds later Rogue saw that he was hanging upside down in a tree.

Seemed like her new mutant friend could add eavesdropping to his abilities.

Seeing Nightcrawler hanging from the tree above them hadn't surprised Jean much. She didn't dislike him. In fact, she found him rather amiable—and saving Rogue had earned him big brownie points.

He blinked rapid blinks from where he sat on the ground across from her.

"I didn't mean to snoop," he said nervously as Storm put a steadying hand on his shoulder.

"Relax," Jean told him. She rested her fingers lightly against his temples. He flinched. His eyes rolled back slightly and his black hair stood on end.

Jean concentrated hard. Blurry flashes from Nightcrawler's mind flickered in front of her. Her body trembled, taking them in.

Flash! Soldiers holding Nightcrawler on the ground. *Flash!* Nightcrawler held in the back of a truck. *Flash!* Entering a long, dark tunnel. *Flash!* A massive laboratory in front of him. *Flash!* A camera flash going off.

Exhausted, Jean pulled away. She'd absorbed enough to tell her what she needed to know. "Stryker's at Alkali Lake," she told the others.

"That's where the professor sent me," Logan said resolutely. "There's nothing left."

Jean looked at him. "There's nothing left on the surface, Logan. The base is underground."

—X2—

Logan paced back and forth. Night had settled in, and a thick layer of fog that Storm had created hung over their forest camp. The others were busy finishing setting up camp. But Logan wasn't in any mood to help. He couldn't get past Magneto's words about Stryker. About himself.

"Hey," Jean called from where she stood on the ramp, repairing the X-Jet's underbelly. "You okay?"

Logan joined her. "Yeah. How are we doing?"

"Not good," Jean told him. "It'll take four or five hours before I can get it off the ground."

He looked at her. "That's not what I meant."

Jean sighed. "I'm just worried about Scott."

"I'm worried about you," Logan told her. "That was some display of power up there."

Jean let out a complacent chuckle. "It obviously wasn't enough."

Logan moved closer to her. Her eyes looked even greener than normal tonight.

"I love him," Jean added.

Logan suspected the words were more an attempt to convince herself than actual fact. "Do you?" he challenged, reaching out and touching a stray lock of her red hair.

"Girls flirt with the dangerous guy, Logan, but they don't take him home," Jean said, her face a mixture of pining and resignation. "They marry the good guy."

"I could be the good guy," Logan whispered.

"Logan, the good guy sticks around," Jean came back.

Logan leaned in and kissed her. But it was over before it had barely begun.

"Please," Jean said, breaking away. "Don't make me do this."

"Do what?" Logan asked. He didn't wish any harm to come to Cyclops, but having him out of the picture would make things a lot easier.

Jean didn't answer. Instead, she walked up the ramp.

Logan hung his head. Maybe things were easier. But they sure didn't feel that way.

CHAPTER TWELVE

MASSACHUSETTS AIRSPACE

The X-Jet was high in the orange early-morning sky as Pyro leaned back in his seat, flicking his lighter on and off.

Logan finished zipping up his uniform.

"Where's ours?" Bobby asked, looking at an X-Uniform that hung inside a locker at the back of the jet.

Rogue cast a hopeful glance at Logan.

"On order," Logan replied, shutting the locker. "Should arrive in a few years."

Pyro watched as Magneto and Mystique continued to whisper to each other. "We love what you've done with your hair," Magneto said with an impish wink to Rogue, referring to the incident of a few months ago. Magneto had created a machine as part of a terrorist attack against nonmutants—

a machine that fed on Rogue's mutant power. Pyro had heard the story of how she had been bound to the machine, and how the draining of her powers had left her with a permanent streak of white in her long hair.

It was kind of funny when you thought about it. Pyro smirked as Rogue glared and walked menacingly toward Magneto. She had yanked off one glove before Bobby pulled her away.

Magneto smiled. Then he turned, suddenly aware of Pyro staring at him. Pyro had been watching the powerful mutant more or less the whole time the airplane had been in flight.

"They say you're the bad guy," Pyro told him, studying him.

"Is that what they say?" Magneto said casually, as if what people said didn't matter in the least.

Pyro flicked his lighter on and off, staring at the helmet in Magneto's lap. "That's a dorky-looking helmet. What's it for?"

Magneto gave him a calculated look. "This dorky-looking helmet is the only thing that's going to protect me from the *real* bad guys." With a wave of Magneto's finger, Pyro's lighter was snapped from his hands into Magneto's palm. He flicked it on.

"What's your name?" he asked.

"John," Pyro said.

Magneto smiled slightly. "What's your real name, John?"

Pyro considered what to say. He reached over and touched the small flame, lifting it from the lighter onto his fingertip. He rolled the flame between his fingers like a coin.

"Pyro," he said at last.

"That's quite a talent you have, Pyro," Magneto said admiringly.

"I can only manipulate the fire," Pyro was quick to point out. "I can't make it." He closed his hand and the flame was snuffed out.

"You are a god among insects," Magneto said quietly. "Don't let anyone tell you different." He opened his palm and the lighter floated back into Pyro's waiting hand.

Pyro considered Magneto's words. It was the first time that someone had told him exactly what he wanted to hear.

—X2—

All ten screens were blank. Stryker sat at his desk, watching them for movement. Next to him sat a guard named Wilkins, watching a different set of security monitors. Yuriko stood guard at the door.

Stryker looked up as Lyman entered, flanked by two soldiers. Yuriko moved from her post, stepping in front of them and clenching her fists.

"Your men can wait outside," he told Lyman, who motioned for his men to leave. Satisfied, Yuriko moved back.

"Sir, the machine has been completed to all the specifications," Lyman told him.

"Good."

Lyman glanced around the room. "If I may ask, sir, why are we keeping the children here?"

Stryker flipped a switch. Video monitors showing each of the six children held at the base began to turn on. "I'm a scientist, Mr. Lyman," he said, gazing at the monitors. "When I build a machine, I want to know that it's working."

—X2—

As the X-Jet sat silently in a patch of snowy woods, Storm pointed to yet another area on the holographic terrain map. With the naked eye, all the X-Men could see was snow. That was why maps like this were so important. "This is a topographic map of the area," she said, clicking a button. The map changed into a high-contrast version, displaying a series of marks that represented repetitive impact over time.

Logan peered intently at the map.

"And here are the density changes in the terrain," she continued. "The lighter the mark, the heavier the repetitive activity." A series of lines branched out from the right spillway tunnel of Alkali Base into what looked like hundreds of tire tracks.

"That's the entrance," Logan said, a slight smile forming on his lips.

Storm changed the map once more. Now it showed the spillway and tunnel entrance in shades of blue, with other areas in shades of white. "This shows the depth of the ice that covers the ground. Recent water activity."

Jean pointed. "If we go in here, Stryker could flood the spillway."

Storm turned to Nightcrawler. "Can you teleport inside?"

"I have to be able to see where I'm going," he answered. "Otherwise I could wind up inside a wall."

Storm considered this. She was of more use out here than inside, but—

"I'll go," declared Logan. "I have a hunch he'll want me alive."

Magneto made his way from the back of the jet to join the X-Men, walking through the map as he did so. "Logan, whoever goes inside the dam needs to be able to operate the spillway mechanism. What do you intend to do? Scratch it with your claws?"

Logan shrugged. "I'll take my chances."

"But I won't," Magneto replied. And then he explained his plan.

CHAPTER THIRTEEN

STRYKER'S BASE

The guards in the control room were bored. They were so used to not expecting anybody that they almost missed Logan as he entered the spillway.

"Sir, someone's entered the spillway," Wilkins said. His hand went for the button. "I'm flooding it."

"Wait!" Stryker grabbed his wrist. "Look who's come home," he said under his breath. "Is he alone?"

"Appears to be."

There was no time to waste. Stryker mobilized his men, and within seconds, two soldiers were aiming their weapons directly at the Wolverine.

Stryker had been prepared for a fight, so he was pleasantly surprised when Logan surrendered and soon was bound in shackles with his famous claws pointed toward his own throat.

Having the Wolverine back at Alkali was going to be very interesting in light of recent events.

Moments later, Stryker, Lyman, and Yuriko entered the loading bay. Stryker approached his captive. There was something about him, though, that wasn't quite right. Something in the eyes . . .

"The one thing I know better than anyone else is my own work," he told the others, anger building inside him. "Shoot it."

As fast as lightning Logan transformed into the scaly blue-skinned Mystique. Before anyone realized what was happening, she had slipped out of her shackles, kicked the guards on either side of her, and hurled her shackles at another guard's face.

Landing on the ground, crouched like a spider, Mystique gave Stryker one last look. Then she darted down the corridor.

—X2—

Alarms wailed throughout the complex as soldiers ran to and fro, trying to figure out where the shape-shifter had gone.

"What's happening?" Wilkins shrieked as Stryker and a guard burst into the control room a few moments later.

"We have a metamorph loose," Stryker said. "She could be anybody."

"Anybody?" Wilkins repeated fearfully.

Wham! Mystique elbowed the soldier, ripping his rifle away and slamming Wilkins across the face. The two men slumped to the floor.

Quickly Mystique pressed a button on the console panel, and the control room door began to close. Before the doors shut, Mystique caught a glimpse of the real Stryker, running toward her with Yuriko, Lyman, and a group of soldiers at his heels.

Mystique blew her new twin a kiss.

And the doors slammed shut.

Shape-shifting back into her true form, she fastened a headset to her ear. The security screens were now blank save for those showing the captured children. She pressed a button, and a map of the base replaced images of the children.

From outside the control room, she could hear Stryker cursing, while his men scurried to get something to blow the doors open with. She didn't have much time.

"I'm in," she said, speaking into the staticky radio that connected her with the X-Jet. Then she began navigating through the map in search of the spillway mechanism.

Magneto would be pleased.

—X2—

Stryker stalked back and forth outside the control room, watching as his soldiers attached a series of magnetic explosives around the edge of the door.

Another soldier leaned over to Lyman. "She's opened the loading bay doors," he whispered loudly enough for Stryker to overhear. "More mutants have entered the base."

"How many?" Lyman asked.

"We don't know."

Lyman turned to him. "Should we engage them?"

Stryker tried to fight back the fear that was building inside him. "No. Have the rest of the soldiers meet us outside the machine." He headed down the corridor. "The mutants can't stop anything," he bluffed to Lyman. "In fifteen minutes, they'll all be on their knees."

He could only pray that he was right.

—X2—

The mansion was eerily quiet as Professor X and Cyclops moved through one of its hallways. Helicopter blades whirred in the distance.

"I don't like this," Cyclops said. "Where is everyone?"

The professor rolled to a stop. "See if you can locate the jet and contact Jean and Storm. I'll use Cerebro."

Cyclops nodded, then headed down the hall.

The professor turned toward the elevator. The sound of a little girl crying caught his ear.

"It's all right, you can come out," he coaxed, spotting her in one of the mansion's dark alcoves.

She stood up and stepped forward, tears in her eyes. "Are they gone?" she asked fearfully. Her cheeks were stained with tears, and her long hair lay in matted clumps.

"Yes. Where are all the others?" Professor X asked her.

She shrugged her small, thin shoulders.

"Then I guess we'll have to find them, won't we?" He held out his hand, and together, they walked down the hallway.

When they reached the door to the huge spherical chamber, the professor paused in front of the retinal scanner. It scanned his eyes, then opened.

"Welcome, Professor," Cerebro said.

"Don't leave me alone, please," the little girl pleaded.

Professor X smiled protectively at her. Of course he wouldn't. But this was bound to be a bit overwhelming for her. "Okay . . . you can come inside."

The child's eyes were wide with anticipation.

But they weren't the eyes of a little girl. They were the eyes of the paralyzed, ghoulish Mutant 143. He was in a wheelchair as well, manned by two soldiers.

Professor X had seen Cyclops. A helicopter. An empty mansion. A little girl. What he didn't see was the truth: that all this time, he had been living in an illusion created by Mutant 143.

And that all this time, he had still been in Stryker's base.

Professor X rolled inside the huge chamber, the little girl behind him.

The door to Cerebro slammed shut.

"There," Stryker murmured as he finished dabbing the yellow liquid on the back of Cyclops's neck. At that very moment soldiers were blasting through the double doors that led to the control room, where that nasty Mystique was trying to cause trouble. Stryker scowled. She wouldn't succeed. He bent down and whispered instructions into Cyclops's ear. Then he left the cell and headed into the corridor.

Yuriko and Lyman were waiting there with dozens of troops. "Position your men," Stryker ordered as they strode down the hall. As the soldiers moved into place, Stryker walked down a platform to Cerebro.

Of course, it wasn't quite the same as it had been when it was in the mansion. Stryker had stolen it from its home and transported it here, to his base. A few things might have shifted in the transition. . . . *Dark Cerebro,* as Stryker liked to think of it. On the whole, Stryker was quite pleased. Even more pleasing was the sight of Professor Charles Xavier sitting in front of the platform, staring at the Cerebro helmet.

Stryker walked up behind him and whispered to Mutant 143, who lurked at the back in his wheelchair. Mutant 143 listened, then wheeled over to the professor.

"Is it time to find our friends?" the mutant asked Professor X.

"Yes," he replied, seeing not Mutant 143, but the illusion of the little girl instead.

"All of the mutants? Everywhere?"

Professor X hesitated. Then he nodded. "Oh, yes."

"Good," Mutant 143 said happily.

"Just don't move," the professor instructed, gazing at her.

For a moment, Stryker felt something stir in his chest as he looked at the mutant he had once considered his son. Shame? Compassion? Sadness? He reached out and lightly touched his shoulder. Then the pity party was over. The world was at stake. He spun on his heel and strode up the platform.

Inside Cerebro the professor would be putting on the helmet. Stryker imagined the walls falling away with the Cerebro effect. Seconds later, Xavier would be sitting inside a giant projection of the Earth, twinkling red lights representing the mutant population dotting the landscape.

Stryker paused in the hallway outside Cerebro, listening as a low throbbing hum started and slowly built up speed. Cerebro was warming up. With a satisfied smile, he walked down the hallway with Yuriko. "Kill anyone who approaches," he told Lyman as he departed, the memory of Mystique fresh in his mind. "Even if it's me."

—X2—

Racing against time, Mystique hurriedly pushed a button, and the monitor switched to a map of Stryker's base.

Bam! The door to the corridor buckled and twisted. Her head swiveled as she searched for an escape. But there was none.

Crash! The door ripped away. And Mystique stood face to face with the X-Men. Two guards hovered upside down in the air, caught by Dr. Grey's telekinetic power. With a wave of her hand, she threw them against the door, knocking them unconscious.

Magneto let the mangled door drop and stepped inside.

"Eric," Mystique greeted her boss.

"Have you found it?" he asked.

She nodded toward a power grid on a nearby screen. "A large portion of the energy from the dam has been diverted"—she pointed at the grid—"here, to this chamber."

"Can you shut it down from here?" Storm asked.

"No."

Mystique stood by impassively as the X-Men stared at the grid. A flicker of annoyance struck her as Logan looked up at the monitor. Stryker was moving quickly through one of the corridors.

"Come," she told Magneto. "We have little time."

Jean Grey reached out a hand. "Not without us."

Ignoring her, Mystique leaned over and hit another button. Instantly, images of the children taken from the X-Mansion flashed on the monitors. She looked to Storm.

"My God," Storm whispered. "The children. Kurt?"

Nightcrawler nodded, squaring his shoulders.

"Will you be all right?" Storm asked Jean, glancing at Magneto and Mystique.

"Yeah, I'll be fine," she said.

"Wait," Storm said. "Where's Logan?"

Mystique took note of the look of disappointment that crossed Jean's face. "He's gone."

—X2—

Back in the vestiges of Dark Cerebro, the huge globe slowly rotated, illuminated by the red lights of mutant populations. Professor X felt strangely sad, almost despondent. What exactly had brought him here again? He felt strangely unsettled and uncomfortable.

"That's odd," he said, looking at the little girl. "I can't seem to focus on anyone."

She gave him a small shrug. "Maybe you have to concentrate harder."

In silent agreement, he reached forward and turned one of Cerebro's many dials. Above him, the red lights grew stronger. The warming hum grew louder.

—X2—

With the unlikely companions Mystique and Magneto by her side, Jean flew down the hallway at the base. Suddenly she clamped her eyes shut, concentrating.

"Wait," she instructed, halting. "I feel something. I think it's—"

A large metal doorway slid open.

"Scott!" she cried as the familiar face moved toward her. But almost instantly she realized something was wrong. Gone was the smile and sweet disposition she'd come to love. In its place was an emotionless void. Before she could react, he raised his hand to his visor and fired.

Boooom! Jean shoved Magneto out of the way and hit the ground. Seconds later she was on her feet. "Go!" she urged Magneto and Mystique. "I'll take care of him."

"This is the kind of lovers' quarrel we cannot get involved in," Magneto muttered as they headed off.

This was no lovers' quarrel, Jean realized. Something ghastly had happened to Cyclops. As he reached up to fire again, Jean raised her hand and hurled him through the air, wincing as he slammed against a wall, then dropped over a balcony, his hand grasping the edge.

Barely fazed, Cyclops fired again from below, his beam landing on a Humvee and sending it flying across the hallway.

Jean fell hard on the ground, her headset falling from her ear as she dodged the gigantic vehicle. Then she scrambled to her feet and peered over the balcony. Some sort of massive generator room was situated below, and Cyclops was nowhere to be seen. The sound of whirring gears and motors was all she could hear. "Scott?" she called down fearfully into the darkness.

Gathering her wits, Jean ran down a staircase and entered

the dark room. Electrical generators beeped and whirred in all directions.

Weesht! She spun in the nick of time as a blast shot out from Cyclops's visor. Holding up her hand, she used every bit of strength she had to ward off his beam. An invisible protective wall surrounded her. But it wasn't going to last for long. The beam was powerful enough to send her sliding back across the floor. . . . This was a tug-of-war game that she was likely to lose.

Cyclops adjusted his visor, intensifying his beam. The light was so bright, it made Jean scream with pain. "Please! Don't do this," she begged to any part of Cyclops that could still comprehend what was happening.

Suddenly, a faint glow rippled around her body, pushing back against Cyclops's beam. The energy of the two mutant forces mixed and built until *WHAM!* Bright light exploded around them, knocking a dazed Cyclops to the ground and slamming Jean into a wall. Her leg snapped underneath her.

The energy blast shook the room with the intensity of a high-level earthquake. Generators began to rattle. Debris fell from the ceiling. Cracks began forming in the walls.

Jean jumped as she felt something touch her head.

"It's okay! It's me!" came Cyclops's voice. "It's *me*," he repeated gently.

Jean threw her arms around him. "Jean—I'm sorry," he murmured into her hair.

She breathed in his warm, familiar scent, relief spreading over her. "It's okay. I was afraid I had lost you." They helped each other up. She guessed that her leg was probably broken. But there was something else. . . .

"Scott?" she whispered as they began to walk out of the room. "Something's wrong."

She was blind.

— X2 —

Nightcrawler felt brave as he and Storm walked down the long, dark tunnel. When at last they emerged into the light, he blinked. In front of them lay a deep, round pit. Cameras were fastened to the walls.

He peered down into the pit. At the bottom was a cluster of children. They stared up at Storm and Nightcrawler with tearstained faces.

As the children cried out for help, Nightcrawler immediately transported into the pit's depths. He took a deep, steadying breath as two girls screamed at the sight of him, backing away.

"Come to me," he said, beckoning gently. "It's all right."

A girl stepped forward. Nightcrawler wrapped his arms around her. He couldn't take more than one at a time. "Now close your eyes," he instructed.

Bamf!

CHAPTER FOURTEEN

STRYKER'S BASE— moments later

Logan was on the warpath. He moved stealthily down the corridor, hunting for William Stryker. Then he smelled something. He sniffed the air. On his right was a sign that read MEDICAL PERSONNEL ONLY.

He wasn't one for rules. Logan headed down the stairs. The sight at the bottom made his stomach lurch. It was a large, dilapidated medical laboratory, circular in shape.

Logan wandered through the lab, drinking it in. The room had clearly seen better days. Massive columns supported a large ring in the center that contained a tank of some sort. Trays littered with torturous medical instruments sat on tables. X rays of mutant skeletons of all shapes and sizes hung haphazardly from the walls.

He walked over to the tank. It was filled with an amber-colored liquid. A rack of medical instruments dangled above the tank. Memories flooded over him. *This is the tank. The tank from my nightmares. The tank from my past . . .*

Next to the tank sat a large cylinder filled with a steaming, metallic-looking liquid. Long tubes with syringes attached to them snaked out from its core.

A voice startled him from his ghoulish exploration. "You know, the tricky thing about adamantium is that if you ever manage to process its raw, liquid form, you have to keep it that way. Keep it hot. Because once the metal cools, it's indestructible."

Logan spun around to see Stryker standing at the room's entrance. Next to him was a tall, stone-faced woman. Yuriko.

Stryker walked into the lab. "But you already know that." He studied Logan. "I used to think you were one of a kind, Wolverine. I truly did." He blew out his breath. "I was wrong."

Years of pent-up rage sent Logan charging across the lab, ready to kill the man who had made him who he was.

Whomp! The woman grabbed him, taking him by surprise. She threw him into a pole.

Slowly, Logan got to his feet. Out of the corner of his eye he saw Stryker back into a tunnel and shut the door. No matter. He'd take care of the woman first. Then he'd move on to his next adversary.

Snikt! His claws popped out. The woman didn't flinch. Instead, she held out her arms and spread her fingers wide. *Snikt!* Eight-inch adamantium claws emerged from each fingertip.

Logan gaped in disbelief. "You've gotta be kidding me," he muttered.

Slash! The woman smiled, flicking one long finger against Logan's cheek.

Logan sneered. Then, baring his claws, he moved in for the attack.

It was a fierce battle. Logan swiped at her head, narrowly missing her as she ducked and then came back up and kicked him. He fell hard against a pile of old equipment, barely able to catch his breath before she leaped on top of him, hands slashing the air.

Claws against claws, adamantium against adamantium. Logan was raging. He sidestepped her slashing claws as she lashed out and missed, hitting a cluster of power cables in the ceiling. Electrical sparks fell to the ground.

With a roar, Logan tackled her, crashing them both through a glass wall. X rays and equipment shattered around them. His body was a mixture of pain as her claws shredded his skin, and healing as his body repaired itself. It registered in him that her body functioned the same way his did.

Except one thing was different. She was much, much faster than he was.

So fast that she had kicked and slammed him into the tank before he knew what had hit him. Amber liquid swirled around him.

This is the place. This is the place! Logan was terrified.

The woman jumped onto the tank and raised her claws,

ready to deliver her final death blow. Just as she was about to strike, icy fear propelled Logan directly upright. He grabbed hold of the rack that hung above the tank. Swinging on its top, he sliced the wires that held it in place.

The rack, bearing Logan, crashed down on top of the woman, trapping her inside the tank.

"Noooooo!" she screeched, trying to claw her way out of the makeshift cage.

Logan quickly rolled off and grabbed a handful of the syringes that were attached to the adamantium cylinder. "Unnhh!" he grunted, jamming them through the cage, straight into the woman's chest.

Agonizing screams filled the air as Logan stumbled back, watching as metal oozed out of the woman's eyes and mouth. Seconds later she fell back into the water. The adamantium had cooled and solidified. She was dead. And the tank that had been the site of his creation became a coffin for Stryker's latest creation.

Logan couldn't get out of there fast enough. But as he ran for the exit door, an unbelievable pain shot through his skull.

Wolverine collapsed in front of the door, his aching head in his hands.

Cerebro was humming, throbbing at a deafening level. Lyman and the guards who were on duty outside the chamber could barely hear one another. Lyman almost missed the slight rattling sound on his person. He had a grenade on his belt. And the pin was rattling. Vibrating.

All of the guards' grenade pins were shaking.

There was only a split second of realization. Then Magneto used his power to yank the pins out en masse and *kaboom!*

Magneto and Mystique waited for the smoke to clear. Then they walked down the hallway, dropping grenade pins to the ground.

—X2—

Inside Cerebro, the world map rotated at a dizzying pace, thousands of mutant-indicator lights spinning. The low, throbbing hum grew faster and faster. Suddenly, a burst of light flooded the map. And then the horror began.

—X2—

Jean Grey's blind eyes were wide with terror as a chorus of voices flooded her mind.

"Jean, what's wrong?" Cyclops cried.

She could barely form a sentence. "It's Cerebro. We're too

late." By then the pain was too much. She collapsed, holding her head, as millions of whispers and screams overwhelmed her mind. And as the earsplitting throb of Cerebro filled the room, Cyclops clutched his visor and fell beside her.

—X2—

Nightcrawler and Storm were on their way to safety with the children. They didn't make it. The deep, resonant droning of the Cerebro signal pierced their ears, making the children drop like flies. Nightcrawler tried to help them. But with Storm contorted on the floor in front of him, her eyes milky white, and a relentless pain attacking his head, Nightcrawler found himself falling to his knees. Thunder crackled above. But there was nothing either of them could do.

—X2—

Make it stop. Make it stop! Logan thought, writhing on the floor of the lab. It was a blaring, deafening throb. *Am I going to die in the same room I was created in?* he thought, half-crazed. Then he could think no more.

—X2—

Back in the X-Jet, Rogue and Bobby were too weak to move. They lay crying on the aircraft's floor. Bobby reached out and grabbed Rogue's hand, squeezing it tightly. Tears flowed from his eyes, mingling with the tears caused by the Cerebro signal.

—X2—

Pyro had set off on his own. Now he curled up alone on the cold forest floor, hyperventilating as the snow around him melted into puddles.

—X2—

Mystique couldn't control herself. Her body twisted into a horrible compilation of all the people she had ever copied. "Eric, hurry," she managed to say as Magneto approached Cerebro's door. She glimpsed Magneto lifting his hand. The sound of metal scratching metal filled the air. The pain was still agonizing. But Cerebro's throb began to slow.

Magneto concentrated, his hand trembling. A magnetic wave rippled through the corridor. There was a deafening throb. And then . . . nothing.

Utter silence.

It was over.

CHAPTER FIFTEEN

STRYKER'S BASE—
later that day

Magneto waved his hand, opening the door to Cerebro. Stepping inside, he saw Professor X sitting comatose in front of the console.

"That's strange," Xavier mumbled to himself, unaware of his visitor.

"Hello, Charles," Magneto said, walking down the long platform. He came to a stop in front of Mutant 143, who sat behind his old friend. "How does it look from there, Charles? Still fighting the good fight?" He clucked his tongue. "From here, it doesn't look like they're playing by your rules."

Professor X looked dizzily around the room that he believed to be the X-Mansion. He could vaguely hear Magneto's voice.

Magneto raised his arms as if he were conducting an

orchestra. "Maybe it's time to play by theirs." With a flick of his wrist, Cerebro began to reconfigure. Ceiling panels, metal braces, tubes, and wires soared through the air in a swirl of metal and movement. When all was restored, he lowered his arms.

Mystique came quietly into the chamber. She looked at Magneto. And then she shape-shifted into William Stryker. It was in this new form that she walked up to Mutant 143 and whispered into his ear, "There's been a change of plans."

"Good-bye, Charles," Magneto said.

Professor X nodded foggily, closed his eyes, and put the Cerebro helmet on his head.

Billions of white lights flooded the globe, each light representing the nonmutants of the world. The rest of humanity. And, thanks to Magneto and Mystique, Cerebro's new targets.

—X2—

Stryker had emerged from an escape tunnel into the bright daylight of Alkali Base. The rusted, decayed dials in the maintenance room had told him that the bursting of the dam was a certainty. He wasn't about to stick around to witness it. After trudging through the snow, he'd climbed over a hill and through a patch of trees. At the forest's edge, a helicopter sat waiting.

He hurriedly began unchaining it from a series of posts, preparing it for takeoff. Tossing the final chain aside, he rounded the side of the helicopter and *SMASH!* A fist made of metal crashed into his face.

It was Logan. The Wolverine.

For some reason Stryker chuckled, staring curiously at Wolverine as he yanked him to the ground. "Why did you come back?" he asked, blood running from his nose.

"You cut me open," Wolverine gritted out. "You took my life."

Stryker scoffed at him. "You make it sound as though I stole something from you. As I recall, it was you who volunteered for the procedure."

"Who am I?" Wolverine shouting, seething.

Stryker stepped back. "You're just a failed experiment." His eyes narrowed. "If you really knew about your past, what kind of person you were, the work we did together . . . People don't change, Wolverine," he told him, his voice acerbic. "You were an animal then, and you're an animal now. I just gave you claws."

Back inside the base, the X-Men and the children came to life again, the horrible sound that had almost killed them gone silent. With the children and Nightcrawler by her side, Storm approached the door to Cerebro. A new, different hum was building.

Nightcrawler's eyes blinked rapidly. "What is this?"

Storm didn't try to quell the fear quivering inside her.

"Cerebro." To her relief, Jean and Cyclops came running around the corner. "Jean, what's happening?" she cried. "Where's Magneto?"

Jean shook her head. "I don't know." She stepped forward, her forehead creasing. "The professor is still inside . . . with another mutant. He's trapped in some kind of . . . illusion." She was quiet for a second. "Magneto's reversed Cerebro. It isn't targeting mutants anymore."

"So who's it targeting?" Storm asked, frightened.

The blood had drained from Jean's face. "Everyone else."

Cyclops reached for his visor. "Stand back."

"Scott, no," Jean said, stopping him. "Once the professor's mind is connected to Cerebro, opening the door could kill him."

"We have to take that chance," Cyclops insisted.

Sweat dotted Storm's neck. "Scott, wait." Cold realization hit her. It was up to her. "Kurt, I need you to take me in there. Now."

Cyclops balked. "Storm, who is this guy?"

"I'm Kurt Wagner," Nightcrawler began graciously. "But in the Munich circus—"

"He's a teleporter," Storm cut in breathlessly.

Nightcrawler took a deep, exaggerated breath. *"I told you. If I can't see where I'm going—"*

"I have faith in you," Storm said, staring meaningfully into his frail yellow eyes.

Something inside him clicked, and he looked back at her

with renewed determination. Then he nodded, wrapping his arms around her.

"Don't believe anything you see in there," Jean warned.

Storm nodded, closing her eyes and bracing herself for the worst.

"If you're not out in five minutes, I'm coming in after you," Cyclops said firmly.

Then, with Nightcrawler whispering the words to the Lord's Prayer in Storm's ears, *bamf!* they teleported into Cerebro.

—X2—

When she opened her eyes, there was only darkness. There was no Cerebro helmet or console. Cerebro wasn't activated. And there was no Professor X.

Instead, there was a little girl, standing in solitude at the edge of the platform.

Nightcrawler's eyes darted nervously around the chamber. "As it is in Heaven?" he said cautiously, then finished the rest of his prayer.

The little girl smiled at them. "Hello."

Storm felt Nightcrawler grasp her arm. "Storm . . . this is Cerebro?"

She nodded.

"Is it broken?" he asked.

"No," Storm said quietly.

"What are you looking for?" the little girl asked them.

"Professor!" Storm shouted out, ignoring her. She knew, felt, that the X-Men's leader was here, inside Cerebro. Probably in his own illusion. Did it include a thin little girl? Storm wasn't going to waste time finding out.

"I'm sorry," the little girl said, her voice high and tinny. "He's busy."

Storm walked toward her. "Professor, can you hear me? You're in an illusion." She drew a deep breath. "You have to stop Cerebro now."

The little girl shook her head, an amused smile on her lips. "Who are you talking to?"

Nightcrawler began to walk toward her. Storm stopped him. "Kurt. Don't move."

"She's just a little girl," Nightcrawler insisted, as if she were as harmless as a kitten.

"No, she's not," Storm told him.

Nightcrawler's eyes widened. "Oh."

The little girl nodded. "Good advice."

Storm wasn't sure what to do next. She exchanged a look with Nightcrawler, then stood there, uncertain.

"I've got my eyes on you," the little girl whispered spookily.

Suddenly a tremendous explosion rocked the base—and Cerebro. The illusion that Storm and Nightcrawler were living in quickly dropped, revealing huge white lights and a terrible, wrenching sound. Cerebro was humming, active, and alive. Storm recoiled as the little girl faded and she saw

Professor X sitting next to a horrible, ghoulish mutant. In a blink, a peaceful calm took over. The illusion was back.

So was the little girl. Her eyes were dark. And angry.

—X2—

Logan could hear the dam's siren in the distance. "What the hell is that?" he shouted at Stryker. "What is it?" he repeated when he got no answer.

"The dam is ruptured," Stryker said knowingly. "It's releasing water into the spillway, trying to relieve the pressure . . . but it's too late." He smirked resignedly. "In a few minutes we'll *all* be underwater."

Logan looked back at the escape tunnel. *Not if I can help it.*

"Still want answers?" Stryker went on. "I'll tell you everything. You're a survivor, Wolverine. You always have been."

"I thought I was just an animal." Without warning, *snikt!* he pressed a claw against the man's throat. "With claws." He pressed them hard against his opponent's weaselly neck, barely able to keep himself from making bloody gouges all over the man's skin.

Then a familiar voice echoed in his head. *Logan, where are you?*

Logan looked up. "Jean," he whispered. What was he going to do? Stryker held the key to his past. But his friends, the

141

X-Men, held the key to his future. And without his help, they would die, trapped underground.

"There's only one way out of here, Wolverine," Stryker said, jarring him. "Come with me and you'll live. Go back there and you'll all die."

Snikt! Logan's claws retracted. He grabbed a chain that had once anchored the helicopter, and tied a panicked Stryker to a pylon. "If we die, you die." Then he raced back to the tunnel.

"There are no answers that way, Wolverine!" Stryker yelled out in anger.

Logan never turned back.

—X2—

Professor X was almost certain he heard something. A faint whisper among the millions of voices crowding his brain. He strained to listen. "Did you hear that?" he asked the little girl.

She shook her head.

But he was sure of it. The whisper floated around him, then up through the sky. "I hear them, but I can't find them," he murmured, feeling helpless.

"Then concentrate harder," the little girl told him.

Professor X nodded. He turned a few knobs on Cerebro's panel. And then he closed his eyes.

All over the world, nonmutants closed their eyes as a tremendous pain surged through their heads.

Tourists sunbathing on the beaches of Hawaii.

Office workers hunched over their computers in Philadelphia.

Skiers on the snowy slopes in Austria.

Grade school children playing tag in London.

The president of the United States.

All lay clutching their heads in agony. All of them dying.

Among them was Stryker, still chained to a pylon. He trembled now, fear and pain washing over his face. He tugged futilely at his chains, on the very brink of consciousness. He was almost gone when he heard a voice.

"It appears there was something wrong with Cerebro. But don't worry. I fixed it."

Stryker managed to lift his head up to see Magneto and Mystique stepping toward him. Magneto was laughing.

"Mr. Stryker, it seems that we keep running into each other."

Whip! The chains around Stryker tightened and began to pull him away from Magneto. The Master of Magnetism smiled. "Mark my words, it will never happen again."

As Stryker's body was dragged away, Magneto turned toward the helicopter cockpit. "Survival of the fittest, Mr. Stryker," he said.

The little girl looked far too happy for Storm's peace of mind. "He'll be finished soon," the child said, grinning. "It's almost time." The words sent a chill down her spine.

Storm turned to Nightcrawler. There was *no* more time. She had to do something now. "Kurt, it's going to get very cold in here," she warned.

Nightcrawler planted his feet firmly. "I'm not going anywhere."

Storm stared at the little girl. Her eyes went white.

"What are you doing?" the little girl asked, confused.

Storm could hear Nightcrawler's teeth rattling. She was sure he was shivering and shaking as well. Of course he would be. The air was reaching arctic temperatures.

Storm concentrated with all her might. She wished Nightcrawler had one of his blankets, because it was going to get a lot colder.

"Stop it!" the little girl burst out, her arms wrapped around herself. "Nooooo!" she screamed. "No!"

And then something happened. Storm's icy storm caused the illusion to melt down around them. Soon they were standing in the middle of a brightly lit Cerebro, the chamber alive with the force of billions of pulsating white lights. The noise was deafening.

Professor X sat in his wheelchair, his stoic face covered with frost, the helmet on his head. Behind him, where the little girl had stood, sat a man slumped in another wheelchair, his breath visible in the air. Storm knew he was the mutant behind the illusion.

The professor lifted his head and opened his eyes, blinking. "Jason?" he said, turning slowly toward the mutant.

"No!" the mutant cried, shielding his eyes.

For the first time Professor X looked up and noticed the lights. Instantly, he closed his eyes and removed his helmet.

The lights faded. The hum stopped.

Storm felt her eyes go back to normal. She watched as the professor extended his hand toward the mutant.

Then a tremendous explosion rocked the chamber. The dam was collapsing. Ceiling plates and girders shattered around them, burying the mutant called Jason. Storm gasped as a giant chunk of debris plummeted toward them.

Bamf! Bamf! Beams and rafters smashed into the chamber—and into Professor X's now-empty chair. Empty because Nightcrawler had saved them.

Magneto settled into the helicopter cockpit next to Mystique. They were just about to take off when he noticed her looking outside. He followed her gaze to see a lone figure standing in the woods, flicking a lighter.

Pyro.

Magneto glanced at Mystique, who gave an almost imperceptible shrug. With a smile and an encouraging nod, he beckoned to the young man.

As the propellers spun, Pyro hesitated, then put the lighter into his pocket and walked toward the helicopter.

As the new threesome took off, Magneto eased back in his seat, a feeling of purpose settling over him. The angry young mutant with the ability to manipulate fire would be a solid addition to his team.

They would be a brotherhood, united in a common goal.

Mutant superiority had not yet been achieved.

But as the helicopter rose above the horizon, Magneto felt certain that their day would come.

Dust spattered from the ceiling as Logan jammed his metal claws into the loading bay's control switch. The huge spillway tunnel doors slammed shut just as the rest of the X-Men rounded the corner.

"Trust me, you don't want to go in there," Logan said, thankful that he was able to stop them from entering, when *BOOOOOM!* what sounded like a tremendous earthquake rocked the room, slamming the newly shut doors. As the doors shuddered, a trickle of water leaked through the seam.

It was as Logan had feared—the spillway had flooded. And the pressure building in the tunnel would have killed the X-Men if he hadn't shut the doors in time. Even worse was what he knew would be happening in the dam . . . cracks spreading like spiderwebs, chunks of concrete beginning to fall away. By the sound of what had just had happened, he figured the entire dam was about to go any minute.

He retracted his claws. "Come on," he ordered. "There's another way out."

Logan and the X-Men raced through a passageway that led outside. They scrambled up the hill looming in front of them, where a few children had made their way to safety. Then they turned back to watch in horror.

Chunks of concrete peeled away from the building like warming blobs of Jell-O. Hundreds of thousands of gallons of water erupted through the opening and crashed into the forest.

One of Professor X's students tugged on Logan's arm. "What is that?" he asked, eyes wide with fear as the trees around them began to shake.

"Alkali Lake," Logan said as the sound of snapping wood echoed in the distance. "All of it." Then a rumble from behind him grew to a crescendo . . . and the massive form of the X-Jet came crashing through the forest and soared unsteadily into the air above them.

CHAPTER SIXTEEN

THE X-JET

Rogue clutched the plane's landing gear, petrified. Land and snow and trees rushed by her in a blur of white as she looked out the windshield and fought desperately to maintain control of the giant aircraft. Fear made her push too hard and fast on the control stick. She and Bobby had tried desperately to come up with a plan after Pyro had abandoned them, leaving them alone with their worry and inexperience. Flying the plane to rescue the X-Men had seemed like a good idea. A heroic one.

Until she actually tried it.

Gripping the controls, Rogue screamed as the plane slammed into a woodsy snowbank.

Stunned, Rogue gaped out at the wintry scene in front of

her. She took a deep breath. If she could see snowflakes and icicles, she was still alive. From beside her, Bobby gave her shoulder a quick squeeze.

"Hurry!" Bobby called, pressing the button to extend the ramp. He dashed out and waved the X-Men inside while Rogue swallowed the lump of fear that had set up home in her throat.

Storm boarded the plane and slid quickly into the cockpit beside her. "It's okay," Storm whispered. "You can let go."

Rogue forced herself to unglue her knuckles from the controls. Her legs were shaking as she headed to the back of the X-Jet and Logan claimed the seat that had been hers.

"Thrusters four and six are out," Storm announced as Rogue took an empty seat. The engine power rumbled on, then off again. The engines whirred and strained in the snow-bank.

"We should still be able to fly," Cyclops said.

"There's not enough power to pull us out of the ground," Storm said worriedly.

Rogue fumbled with a seat belt as the plane began to tremble with the effects of the oncoming power. She looked over to see Dr. Grey, her eyes closed, obviously concentrating hard.

Rogue clasped her hands together. Her lips were dry. She had come to her friends' rescue, but if they couldn't get the plane off the ground, they'd be smashed to bits. Or drowned. Images of water and flailing limbs swarmed in her brain.

Until she realized that the control panel was lighting up. Switches and dials were turning by themselves. And then the flight controls pulled back, the pedals pushed in, and thrusters flaring, the X-Jet slowly started to rise.

Dr. Grey's powers were amazing! As the roar of the engine came on full blast, Storm grabbed the controls and pulled. "Thrusters are back online!"

Rogue pressed her face against the window. The X-Jet rose above the snow-covered forest as billions of gallons of water—an icy wave—crashed down on the clearing they had just departed. Within seconds, Alkali Base was submerged.

Rogue turned her weary head, resting it against the plush headrest. She watched quietly as Logan solemnly removed his dog tag from his neck, gave it a long stare, then put it into his pocket.

She yawned sleepily, the day's events suddenly overwhelming her. Maybe Logan could finally come to terms with his past. Whatever happened, she hoped that his future would be with them. The X-Men.

As Rogue drifted off, the X-Jet soared upward, disappearing into the clouds.

THE WHITE HOUSE

"In this time of adversity, we are being offered a unique opportunity," President McKenna said resolutely, staring into the TV camera that was filming his presidential address to the nation. "A moment to recognize a growing threat within our own population."

His staff and Secret Service agents were watching closely from the sidelines. "I have in my possession evidence of a threat born in our own schools," he went on, his fingers grazing the files that William Stryker had given him. He was about to continue when dark storm clouds outside the windows of the Oval Office caught his attention. Lightning flashed and thunder rumbled through the early-afternoon sky. Sheets of rain began to strike the windows.

"A threat we must learn to recognize in order to combat it." The president tried to continue.

Zzaappp! All of the TV monitors in the room went to static. The cameras turned off.

The president looked around him. He was used to commanding attention, but not this much. Everyone in the room was completely motionless. His chief of staff was pouring a glass of water that was now overflowing onto the table. Secret Service agents were frozen in place. A staff member was caught mid-sneeze.

President McKenna's gaze drifted over a sea of still people, landing on a group at the back of the room. A young man wearing a red visor. A tall red-haired woman. A rough, hairy man with stubble on his cheeks. A dark-skinned woman with white hair and all-white eyes. A young girl with long brown hair spilling about her shoulders. All of them wearing matching black leather uniforms. All of them unequivocally staring at him.

A bald man in a wheelchair dressed in a dark black suit broke out of the group and approached him. "Good afternoon, Mr. President."

"Who are you people?" the president shouted, furious. How dare they come in and interrupt his speech like this!

"We're mutants," the man in the wheelchair said. "But we're not here to harm you. My name is Professor Charles Xavier. Please sit down."

"I'd rather stand," the president said harshly, not sure he believed one word of what this man said.

The tall woman moved slightly, and suddenly a folder of files floated over to the president's desk. Stunned, he sat down.

"These are the files from the private offices of William Stryker," Professor X explained.

The president flipped through them, surprised to see that there was some very interesting information contained there. "How did you get these?" he asked.

The man smiled. "Let's just say I know a little girl who can walk through walls."

"I've never seen this file," the president sputtered, incensed.

"I know," Professor X replied.

"Then you also know I don't respond well to threats," President McKenna lashed back.

"This isn't a threat, Mr. President," Professor X corrected him. "This is an offer." He went on. "I realize you may have information about me. About my school. About our people." He paused. "I'm willing to trust you, Mr. President, if you're willing to return the favor. There are forces in this world, mutant and human alike, who believe that a war is coming. You'll see from those files that some have already tried to start one. If we expect to preserve peace, we have to work together."

The president's eyes flickered over the frozen people in the room, and over the files, then back to Professor X's earnest face.

"Do you understand?" the mutant asked him.

The president studied the professor for a moment in silence. "Yes, I think I do."

Professor X looked relieved. "I'm glad. We are here to stay, Mr. President. The next move is yours."

President McKenna looked down at the files the mutant had given him. With a sigh, he pushed aside the old files and put the new ones in front of him. A moment later he looked up—and the X-Men were gone.

Back to the X-Jet.

Ready to defend humankind, mutants and nonmutants alike.

THE eXtraordinary SEQUEL YOU'VE BEEN anXiously eXpecting—BASED ON THE eXciting ALL-NEW MOVIE!

X-MEN 2 ™

A novelization by Chris Claremont
based on the motion picture screenplay
Story by Bryan Singer & David Hayter and Zak Penn
Screenplay by Dan Harris & Mike Dougherty

They're back! Those special few who possess amazing, superhuman abilities. Are they the next step in mankind's evolution...or an entirely new species? Will those among them who seek to live in harmony, and those who strike out with murderous force, ever make peace? And when an insidious new enemy arises, will anyone—mortal or mutant—survive?

And don't miss the eXplosive original adventure— based on the first hit film:

On sale now in paperback

DEL REY A Division of Ballantine Books
Visit us at www.delreydigital.com